Lady in the Woods
Short stories for adults

Penny Luker

First Published in 2021 by Bindon Books, Leyton, Cheshire, CW6 9JA
Printed by Amazon.

Copyright © 2021 Penny Luker

All rights reserved. Penny Luker has asserted her right under the Copyright, Design and Patents Act 1988 to be identified as the author of this work. No part of this book may be reproduced, stored in a retrieval system, or transmitted in any form, without the written permission of the publisher's named above.

All characters in this book are entirely fictional and any resemblance to any living person is entirely coincidental.

Acknowledgements

Many thanks to everyone who has encouraged and helped me to write this book. Thanks to Winsford Writers for ideas; to my fellow writers and family for helping to proof read the book and identifying points to ponder and to my husband David for his support.

ISBN: 9798489083560

Contents

Care	4
A Life Of Her Choosing	11
An Unromantic Tale	16
The Other Side Of The Road	20
Colour Change	26
Reunion	30
A Family Holiday	33
I Remember, I Remember	36
The Plan	47
See How You Run	50
The Following Day	53
Single	56
Curtain Crescent	61
Unexpected Inheritance	66
The Long Driveway	69
The Trouble With Weasels	73
Martha's Dilemma	77
Family Ties	81
The Ring of Mystery	85
Ambition	88
Incomplete	94
September Time	97
Lady in the Woods	105

Care

Inspector Winsford swallowed two paracetamol as he entered the retirement flats. The heat hit him and then the quietness. He hated these places always preferring to be outside. The door of number twenty-six was already open.

He nodded to Constable Staples, who said, 'The carer, Sally Carter, found the body. She's in the kitchen. Very shocked and upset, Boss.'

In the living room, Ethel Evans was slumped in her armchair, head lolling backwards as if she was having a nap. There were no obvious signs of violence, he noted. It looked like a natural death; after all the old girl was ninety four. His head was still thudding as if someone had taken a hammer to his skull. He shouldn't have opened that bottle of whisky last night, but it deadened the pain of his wife leaving him. His mind was drifting. He must concentrate.

The only thing that surprised him about this death was how upset the carer was. Didn't seem to think that Mrs. Evans' death was on the cards at all.

He decided to go and have a chat to her in the kitchen, where she was being given a cup of tea.

The forensic team made their arrival heard, so he left them to it. The flat was frowsty in the way many old people's places are, but in spite of that, everything was neat and tidy.

'Good morning, Miss Carter. I'm Inspector Winsford. When was your last visit to Ethel Evans?'

Sally looked up, cradling her mug. 'I've been off work, sick. The agency sent someone to cover.'

Inspector Winsford repeated the question.

'It was yesterday morning. I gave her breakfast and then got the cramps so I had to go. Caught the blasted thing off my daughter, who got it from school - Rose Hill Primary. They're always passing round colds and bugs. Anyway, I rang my boss and told her I was going home. She said she'd send someone else.'

'Thank you Sally. I'd like you to stay here for a moment. It shouldn't be too long.'

Going back into the living room, he watched Doctor Morgan leaning over the body. If he didn't feel faintly nauseous, he might have tried flirting with her, but one he'd forgotten how and two, at the moment he needed fresh air and some food.

'Well Doc, natural causes, was it?'

Without turning she replied, 'Almost certainly not! I'd guess she's been dead about twenty-four hours. I'll confirm that when I get her to the lab. I found this in her left nostril,' she said waving an evidence bag containing a tiny white feather. 'I'll be doing a post mortem this afternoon, Winsford, but it looks like we've got ourselves a murder.'

Inspector Winsford sighed and went back to the kitchen. More questions needed to be asked.

'Well Sally, it seems I need more information,' he said taking a piece of paper and pen and handing them to her. 'Please write down the agency you work for, who you phoned and the number and tell me did you use your own phone or Mrs. Evans' landline?'

Sally put down her mug onto the clean but scratched Formica topped table and picked up the pen.

'I used my phone.'

'And what time did you make the call?'

'It was about ten thirty.'

Inspector Winsford stayed quiet and Sally filled the silence. 'I arrived at ten fifteen and made her breakfast; just tea and toast. I have half an hour on a Monday morning to make her breakfast and put the washing on. Normally I'd be back at lunchtime to microwave a ready meal for her and hang the washing out, but as I said I went home ill. I should've been back this morning but I was running late and thought it wouldn't matter if I didn't get in 'til lunchtime. At a push Ethel can get herself a cup of tea.'

Sally handed the paper she'd written on, to the Inspector.

'How was Mrs Evans when you left her yesterday? Was she well?'

'She was fine. It was me who was feeling ill. She was chirpy and chatty. Nice lady. I certainly wasn't expecting her to pass away yet. Normally you can tell.'

'Unfortunately, it looks like Mrs Evans didn't die naturally, Sally. If you have anything you want to tell me, now would be a good time.'

Sally's face drained of colour. 'I didn't hurt her,' she whispered, obviously struggling to speak.

Inspector Winsford yawned as he left the building and drove the five minutes down the road to the Warren Care Agency. At least he felt better being out of that dreadful flat. His head was now muzzy rather than painful.

Entering the functional but unglamorous offices of the agency he found Bethany Prout painting her nails with strange designs. He couldn't help but contrast the slightly plump Miss Prout with Sally Carter. The latter was short, thin and pretty in an elfin way, wearing flat plain shoes and an unflattering blue overall. Bethany, on the other hand, wore a too short leather skirt, black tights and lethal heels. When she stood up, he estimated her to be nearly six feet.

He flashed his ID and explained why he was there.

'Sally Carter says she called you around ten thirty yesterday and you arranged cover because she was sick.'

'Oh, she did, did she? Well, she's lying. We've had a lot of trouble with her not turning up on jobs. I should've put her on a warning really but I'm too soft,' she smiled.

'Surely that means that vulnerable adults are being put at risk?'

'No. All our carers know that they have to make sure the clients are looked after. If they take a few short cuts, I don't make too much of a thing about it as long as the old folk are fed. Very difficult to get good staff you know.'

'So, let's be very clear; you're saying that you didn't receive a call yesterday from Sally Carter.'

'No, I didn't. Absolutely not.'

'And you didn't know that Mrs Evans needed care arranged?'

'How could I know?'

'Well thank you for your time. I'm just letting you know that I may need to talk to you again. Oh, and can I have the contact details of your other staff?'

'I don't know. That's confidential.'

'Miss Prout this is a murder investigation. Why wouldn't you want to cooperate?'

Silently she stood up and went and pulled out a copy of the staff list from a metal cabinet, trying not to mess her nails up in the process.

Give me strength thought Winsford.

It was time to return to the office. He needed coffee and a sandwich. Once his needs were met, he reviewed the facts with his Sergeant, Chris Willis.

'One of them is lying. Either Sally made the call or she didn't. I want you to phone them up and tell each of them that we're sending for their phone records and offer them the opportunity to change their stories. One of them might crack before we actually have to check the records, which will save us time and money. While you're doing that, I'll be visiting Ms Carter's kid's school. See if her mum was sick yesterday.'

'Shouldn't you have her permission to talk to her child, Sir?'

'The school are in loco parentis. I'll make sure a member of staff is present. Not like I'm going to interrogate her, is it?'

Chris shrugged, walked over to his desk and picked up the phone.

Tracy Carter was small for seven. Her eyes were wide and searching as she was brought into the Head Teacher's office.

'Now Tracy sit down next to me,' said the Head in a gentle voice. 'This gentleman is going to ask you a few questions and that's all right because I'm with you.'

The little girl looked anything but reassured. Best get this over quickly before the Head changes her mind.

'I'm just a bit concerned about your mum,' said Winsford. 'Someone told me she was ill yesterday. Is that right?'

Tracy smiled, looking relieved. 'No, Mum was good yesterday. Uncle Michael was round our place. He's not really my uncle. He's Mum's friend but he's nice. I think Mum had the day off work. She was all dressed up pretty, not ill. He brought me to school this morning.'

'Thank you, Tracy. I'm so relieved your mum's well. Thank you.'

On the way back to the office he called in to get someone to go and pick up Sally Carter. She'd definitely lied about being ill. Who'd have thought she'd commit murder, but you never could tell? She certainly had the means and opportunity but what on earth was her motive?

It had been a long day so far and he hoped he could get away early. At least, since he'd eaten, the headache had finally gone.

As he arrived in the office he found Willis waiting for him.

'Sally Carter did phone in,' he said. 'Bethany Prout changed her story immediately I told her we were checking her phone records and P.C Staples has found three carers who say she contacted them, asking that they cover Sally's shifts. I took the liberty of calling her in and she'll be here shortly.'

Winsford scowled. He would not be going home early tonight.

'Well done, Willis. Good work,' he said and proceeded to update him on his discovery.

They interviewed Bethany first. Her eyes were like a panda's, as her mascara had smudged. She was picking at one of her multi coloured nails as they entered the room. Sergeant Willis cautioned her and offered her a solicitor, which she declined.

'It's Sally's fault really,' she whined. 'I'm in charge. I'm not meant to do the care. I tried to get cover for Sally but none of the girls could do it, so I went round. I didn't mean to hurt her.'

'Tell us what happened, Miss Prout.'

'She said her meal was still frozen and then she said I was useless. She said something like Sally always serves my dinner on a plate and not in the plastic container. Well, how was I supposed to know that? I don't use a plate at home. Saves the washing up.'

Both officers looked at each other but kept silent and she continued.

'Anyway, I took her meal off her and threw it in the bin and she said she was going to complain about me. I told her to go ahead as I was the boss it didn't bother me. And then she said she would be complaining to the council. I'd have lost my agency license. So, I picked up a cushion and held it over her face until she stopped moaning. When I realized what I'd done I took the meal out of the bin and left. She won really, didn't she? My agency will be closed.'

Inspector Winsford stood up and stretched his arms. 'Charge her Sergeant and when you've done that give Ms Carter a stern warning about lying to the police. As if we'd care about her throwing a sicky in the circumstances. I'm off home.'

The thought of a good malt was tempting but he knew at some point he must give it up.

A Life of Her Choosing

Rose rubbed the butter into the flour, but her mind was elsewhere. She felt like Cinderella, stuck in the kitchen. When she finished making the pie there were all the vegetables to prepare.

She could hear Mistress Elizabeth's screams from the room above. What was her friend going through? Unconsciously she pressed the palm of her hand against the gold pendant Elizabeth had given her on her wedding day.

'It's for a rainy day. It'll give you some security,' Mistress Elizabeth had said, although she'd already given her some security. Sir Albert Mansfield, manufacturer and purveyor of fine linen, had needed a cook and Elizabeth had persuaded her future husband that Rose would be cheap and do the job well. It had seemed a perfect solution so she could stay near Elizabeth, but with little help in the kitchen, the work was hard and the hours long.

Rose's fingers were clogged in the mixture. It was meant to become smoother so she could roll it out, but the fine mottled brown powder rested all around the top of the bowl. She knew a few basic meals that her mother had taught her, but now she needed to improve her repertoire with the help of the old cook's recipe book.

It was only three years ago, when she and Mistress Elizabeth had been fourteen that they'd spent their days running freely across the moors, making dens and skimming pebbles on the lake. Those had been happy days for her. She'd discovered Elizabeth living a lonely existence with a father who gambled away all their money with an unhealthy enthusiasm. Her own mother worked all hours to support the two of them and although Rose did what she could to help, often she had long spells of time on her own. She and Elizabeth had known each other in their childhood from church and now they were drawn together.

One day when out walking they came across the dilapidated Fishers' cottage, which was little more than a room. The two girls did it up as best they could with bits and pieces. They had found an old bucket to collect rain water and patched up the tiny window spaces with odd bits of wood. Inside was dry but dark, but Elizabeth had managed to bring some candles from her home and they spent many a happy hour there. Rose collected fruit and edible titbits from the land.

'Here's some home cooked soup, made from the finest nettles in the county,' Rose said with a mock submissive voice.

'How kind,' said Elizabeth taking a deep sniff at the dish.

They laughed out loud. It tasted bitter and smelled like rotting cabbage.

Over many months Elizabeth taught Rose how to read and write to a passable level. They wrote poetry together and delighted in finding clever rhymes and funny phrases.

'Tell me why no-one comes to this cottage, Rose. Why doesn't someone live here?'

'Make yourself comfortable. It's quite a story.'

Nearly two hundred years ago a man called Edward Fisher, his wife and two children lived here and as far as we know they were happy. He was a carpenter and he was skilled at his job. One day the lord of the manor caught him talking to his daughter and the lord, thinking he was flirting with her, dismissed him from his job. Worse than that he ordered that no-one should employ Edward. The little family did their best to survive. They foraged the moors and countryside for food and just about got by, but try as he might he couldn't get any work. They lasted out the summer, but no-one saw them during the winter. At the end of the winter gradually the townsfolk realized that Mr Fisher was living in the cottage on his own. Nobody knows what happened to the wife and children, but of course people gossip and some said that they could hear them roaming the moors, cursed to stay here forever, because they hadn't lived their full lives.

Mr Fisher was questioned by the lord's clerk and said that his family had died from a chill, but the locals thought he'd murdered them because he couldn't support them. We'll probably never know.

'Oh, that's terrible,' said Elizabeth. 'Didn't anyone think that his wife had left him because she couldn't live like that and perhaps she'd taken the children back to live with her mother or maybe a rich stranger had offered her and the children a home?' The girls giggled at such a romantic ending. 'I like that ending much more.'

'So, you're not afraid of the ghosts?'

'Of course not. Why would they want to hurt us?'

Rose didn't tell Elizabeth about the stones piled behind the cottage. She believed that they marked the wife and children's resting place. On balance she thought it more likely that they had died of a chill as he wouldn't have marked their graves if he'd murdered them.

Sir Albert started becoming a regular visitor at Elizabeth's home as her father took them further and further into debt. When Elizabeth's father suggested that the only honourable way out of their situation was for Elizabeth to accept Sir Albert's hand in marriage, Rose begged her to refuse. Why should Elizabeth have to pay for her father's reckless behaviour, but Elizabeth had acquiesced without a fight. In fairness, Sir Albert's proposal had been considerate. He promised that he'd never beat her, would provide her with a decent home, feed and clothe her and in return all he wanted from her was a child to take over his business. He had offered her all the things that Rose wanted to offer, to protect her. Of course, she wasn't in any position to help Elizabeth. She and her mother were pitifully poor and then with little warning her mother died of the flu. Rose lost her home within days as she had no way to pay the rent.

'Don't worry Rose. I'll find you a home,' Elizabeth had promised and so she had.

Now Rose was confined to the kitchen, with its long oak table and black cast-iron range, but Mistress Elizabeth had the harder task. She was confined to the bedroom to produce an heir for Sir Albert. They were both trapped in this grand but dismal building, with its draughts and echoes.

Rose blocked out the screams as best she could. She wanted to run upstairs and rescue her friend, but there was nothing she could do. Mistress Elizabeth had to give birth and she must produce the next meal on time. To give Sir Albert his due he had paid for the doctor to be present, which for a man, careful with his money, showed some care for his young wife.

Rose shuddered at the thought of the intimacy Elizabeth had to endure with the ancient Sir Albert, but it had been her choice to help her father out of his debts. Sir Albert's saggy, sallow skin repulsed Rose and even at a distance she knew his breath was sour. What a price to pay for a genteel life.

Rose added a small amount of water to the mixture and watched as it miraculously took a more manageable form. Just at that moment she heard the squawk of a baby from the upper floors and relief flooded through her. Perhaps after all everything would turn out all right.

With any luck the decrepit Sir Albert would breathe his last before her friend needed to oblige him again.

Silently she thanked the heavens that she was both plain and poor.

Rose longed to slink upstairs to see her friend but Sir Albert had made it very clear, that although he'd offered her a position, her friendship with his wife was now wholly inappropriate. No matter, she would produce an extra special meal so that Mistress Elizabeth would know she was thinking of her. She started to peel the carrots.

At that moment, Maisy, the upstairs housemaid burst into the kitchen.

'Sir Albert just wants a cold lunch served in 'is study. Mistress Elizabeth lost a lot of blood and has passed on,' she blurted out.

Rose's mouth dropped and she wiped the palms of her hands down her apron.

'You'd best see to it then Maisy, hadn't you? Tell Sir Albert I'm off,' she said untying her apron. 'I'm going to live my life for Mistress Elizabeth and me. There's nothing here for me now.' She took a deep breath. 'I'm going to climb mountains, travel the world and swim in the sea.'

Rose ran upstairs and shoved her meagre possessions and the few coins she'd earned, into her tapestry bag. She wrapped the blanket, her mother had woven from rags, around her coat and crept down the back stairs to the garden door. Tonight she would make for the Fisher's Cottage and tomorrow she'd look for less lonely work, perhaps at the Inn or even teaching.

As she opened the heavy door the breeze whipped the tears from her cheeks and she headed for the moors, with one hand holding her bag and the other grasping her pendant. She was sure she could hear Elizabeth's voice in the wind calling for her.

An Unromantic Tale

Mavis and Natalie were friends, but lived different lives. Mavis tried her best not to be jealous of Natalie, but it was difficult.

'Darling, you should see the magnificent roses Karl bought me last night. I told him he shouldn't spend so much. I mean twenty-four crimson red roses. He's just so generous,' she drooled.

'He must really love you,' Mavis said stoically.

'Oh, he does. I couldn't ask for a better husband. Still, I expect your Derek does lovely romantic gestures too.'

'Yes, of course,' she said, but then when she thought about it, she couldn't think of one example.

That evening, after Mavis had kissed the children good-night, she placed a plate of steak and kidney pudding down in front of Derek. Thick brown gravy trickled round new potatoes, carrots and peas.

He smiled at her. 'That looks grand pet,' he said tucking into the mountain before him.

'I'm glad you like my cooking, but why don't you ever buy me flowers, like Karl does for Natalie?' said Mavis.

"Cos, I don't need to. I don't screw around like he does.'

'Karl doesn't 'screw around' as you so nicely put it. He's devoted to Natalie. He's just so romantic. I can read people you know.'

'If you say so pet,' said Derek. 'By the way, did you know you've got gravy on your chin?' Mavis picked up the tea towel she'd used to carry in the plates and wiped her face.

They continued their meal in silence. When the apple pie and custard was finished Derek cleared the plates away and sent Mavis to sit in the front room while he made the coffee.

Handing her a cup he said, 'I suppose you've been out to lunch with Natalie then. Does it ever occur to you why she has to boast about what a wonderful relationship she and Karl have?'

'She doesn't boast. I pick up things in her conversation. He won't let her go back to work, you know. Says now the children are at school it's time for her to have some 'me' time.'

'I've never heard such a load of old cobblers.'

'Derek, I do wish you wouldn't use that language. It isn't necessary.'

'Sorry dear, but it's utter rubbish. If she goes back to the old firm then his bits of crumpet will see she's not an old dog and he won't get his end away so often.'

'Natalie and Karl would never use such language. He's always so polite and charming. Why I don't think I've ever met up with them when he hasn't given me a compliment. Such a lovely man; you could learn a lot from him,' said Mavis.

'Oh, I'm sure there's a lot he could teach me, but perhaps not the kind of things you'd like me to learn,' said Derek pointing the remote at the television.

They settled down to watch Coronation Street and Mavis reached for her make-up bag and then cleaned her face with make-up remover wipes. She tied her hair in an unflattering pony tail and slavered on night cream. The telephone rang.

'I'll get it,' said Derek jumping up from his chair. Mavis turned down the sound on the television. In the hall she could just hear the conversation.

'No, no I won't...

You can say what you like, but I won't tell lies...

I don't care...

Well, I'm not agreeing, am I? Now I'm going back to watch my programme.'

There was a thud as the phone crashed down.

'Who was that?' asked Mavis.
'No-one of any importance,' said Derek.
'Well, what did they want?'
'Nothing,' said Derek turning up the sound.

Mavis sank back in her chair. It wasn't like her husband to hide things from her. He was an open book; never kept secrets. She looked at him as he watched Sally Webster have yet another row with Kevin. Derek's face was white and his lips had thinned. She decided to keep quiet.

The next day was bright and sunny. The children were up early and unusually got ready for school without any nagging. By twenty to nine she was standing around in the playground waiting for the school day to begin.

'Hi Mavis,' said Natalie, dressed in a cream trouser suit. 'What did you do last night? I thought you might call.'

'We had lunch yesterday. Why would I have called?' said Mavis feeling shabby in her jeans and smock blouse.

'Being on your own,' said Natalie. 'You know, the boys went for a drink. Didn't get back 'til almost midnight.'

'What boys? Sorry I'm not with you.'

'Derek and Karl, dopey. Aren't you awake or something?'

Mavis felt adrenaline power through her veins. What should she say? But she remembered the phone call last night. She'd heard her husband say he wouldn't lie. Neither would she.

'Karl must've meant someone else. Derek was home at the normal time. We spent the evening together. Had steak and kidney pud. Watched Corrie. You know, usual stuff.'

The children waved as they ran off into school and Natalie left in a rush for an appointment.

That night, after Mavis had kissed the children good-night, she placed a plate of fish pie in front of Derek; his favourite meal. Creamy white sauce oozed its way round the broccoli and beans.

'Now that looks tasty,' said Derek, smiling at his wife. She smiled back.

'I picked a few tulips for the table,' said Mavis. 'You were right about not needing to buy me flowers. Our whole garden is filled with them. I'm so lucky.'

The Other Side of the Road

Ella had cleaned the house from top to bottom, given the children their bath and changed into smart black jeans and a deep purple top. She felt good for the first time in weeks and very excited. Jim had agreed to babysit the children while she went for a girlie night out. If she were honest, it was the thought of seeing Jim again that made her heart beat faster, although she always enjoyed spending time with her friends. Perhaps when he saw how well she was coping since he'd left her, he might have second thoughts.

Only half an hour before he was due to arrive the telephone rang.

'Sorry Ella, I'm not coming over tonight. I really can't face it. The thought of getting the girls off to bed, and dealing with them if they won't settle, – well I just can't do it.'

'But you promised to babysit. I'm going out.'

'I've tried to explain before, I just can't do the dad bit. I'm just not ready for it.'

'Well, you are a dad. I don't know how you can let them down. I've told them you're coming.'

'You'll have to un-tell them then, because I'm going out tonight. Bye.' The phone went dead.

Ella sat down. Why on earth did she want him back? He was the most selfish person she knew. So tonight, would be another night sitting on her own with the television. She rang Julie to explain that she couldn't come.

'Right, well we'll all come over to you. We'll have a take-a-way delivered and I'll bring some wine. We'll be there by eight so get the table laid.'

Since Jim had left, Ella had taken her time getting the girls off to bed. She read them stories and cuddled them and they all enjoyed this unhurried part of the day. This evening was no different. She didn't have to rush as her friends weren't coming until later. She warmed the plates and laid the table and set out glasses.

No-one complained about having to come to her house. They ate good food, washed down by some decent wine and had a laugh. Ella, whose life seemed to be on hold, managed to join in and was glad to have a break in routine, even if she hadn't seen Jim. Julie stayed behind at the end of the evening to help clear up.

'You know, hard as it's going to be, you're going to need to get out there. Oh, I don't mean to find a bloke; I know it's too soon for that, but you need to do something for you. Perhaps a little part time job or join a class, but something to get you out of the house so that you're not completely isolated.'

'I know you mean well Julie, but I haven't got a babysitter. Anna starts school in September, but Sophie is still a baby and I don't want her going to nursery yet. Besides they've just lost their dad, they don't need to lose me as well, even if it's only for a short time per week. I love them so much.'

'Of course you do, but you still need contact with adults. What about your mother-in-law? She's always enjoyed being with the children.'

'You have to be joking. She's never liked me and she looks at me as if I'm a nasty taste in her mouth. I had to put up with her when Jim was here, but I don't have to now.'

Ella carried on with the daily routines. She missed Jim's company in the evenings but she changed nappies, did the washing, fed and played with the children and just about kept everything going. Then one Tuesday evening the telephone rang.

'Hello Ella, it's Margaret here. I just wondered how you're getting on.'

'You mean since your son walked out and deserted us.'

There was an uncomfortable silence.

'Ella, I will always love my son; I can't pretend not to, but I'm so sorry about how he's behaving. I don't approve of him avoiding his responsibilities.'

'My children are not a responsibility. They are the most precious and beautiful people in the world.'

'I know, my dear and I love them very much too. I was wondering if you'd invite me round on Sunday. I would really love to see them and if I can do anything to help you must let me know.'

'I don't need your help, Margaret, but you can come to lunch on Sunday. We'll be eating at twelve.'

Although Ella didn't really want to see Margaret, she was surprised at the efforts she went to, so that the day went well. The house was looking good and she made sure she'd ironed her clothes and done her hair so that she looked smart. The children were really excited about Grandma coming, which she supposed was understandable as they only had one grandparent to spoil them.

Margaret played with the children, while Ella served up lunch and then she helped feed Sophie. While Ella cleared the plates away, Margaret took Sophie off to change her nappy. In the afternoon they all went out for a walk in the park and spent some time on the swings and slides.

When the children were snuggled up in bed that evening, Margaret made them both a cup of coffee.

'I know you've always put the children first. I know they're your raison d'être and I've always admired you for how well you look after them, but I want you to let me back into their lives and let me help you with them.'

'I can manage fine thank you, Margaret.'

'Yes, you can but please listen to my proposal. Will you?'

'Proposal? I'll listen, but that's all I'm promising.'

'Obviously you don't want to put Sophie in a nursery, just yet. She's still a baby and you've always liked the idea of leaving the nursery until they're about three, but I could look after her for a couple of days a week and I could pick Anna up from school and then you could get yourself a little job.'

'I don't think so.'

'Before you dismiss the idea, please remember that I'd be doing it for me and not for you.'

'What do you mean?'

'I'm on my own too. I miss seeing them every week. I'd look after them and if you'd prefer it, I could look after them here. It would mean you could start rebuilding your life.'

'And it will work fine until I find myself a boyfriend and then you'll cause problems. I don't want to take up your offer, but you can come round and see them. You are their grandma.'

A look of sadness crossed Margaret's face but she smiled at Ella. 'Come to mine, next Sunday. Jim won't be there and I'll cook for you.'

As she stepped out of the front door she turned back to Ella. 'You're wrong about one thing though; when you find another young man, I'll back you a hundred per cent and I'll still want to be part of yours and the children's lives. You're too young to spend years on your own.'

'Can you believe she expects me to leave my children with her, when her son has dumped us all like we're a bag of rubbish?' Ella asked Julie when she went round for coffee the next day.

'Tell me something, did you trust her to look after the children before Jim started acting like a big schoolboy?'
'Well, I suppose so.'
'So, what's changed? She's always doted the girls and you know they love spending time with her. It'd be good for you to get a little job. Get back out there meeting people.'
'You know your problem, you're always too darned logical,' Ella smiled at her friend.

Ella phoned up the school she had worked for before Anna was born and it turned out they were looking for a part-time teacher to provide non-contact time for the other teachers. This was not the job she would have chosen but it was only for two days a week.
Now she had to face the difficult task of asking for Margaret's help. Margaret who was always so superior and had never thought her good enough for her precious son. She practised asking her in her mind over and over, but it needed to be done. She needed to find a way to build her life over again and this was a way to start. Plucking up the courage she walked the children round to Margaret's house after Sophie's afternoon nap.
Margaret kissed and hugged them all when Ella asked her to have the children so she could go back and teach.
'I'm so excited. I'll never let you down. I can't believe I am so lucky to have a daughter-in-law that I love and the two best grandchildren in the whole world.'
'I have to admit I thought you didn't think very much of me,' Ella braved herself to say.
'On the contrary, I just thought that things might not turn out right and I didn't know what I could do.'

It was five years later that Jim was passing the Registry Office on the opposite side of the road. He had an arm draped around Marlene or was it Tracy. He really couldn't remember; there'd been so many and actually they were all the same. She was chewing gum and mumbling some mindless nonsense about the latest fashion in hair. He recognized Anna first who had linked her arm with his mum and then he remembered that it was today that Ella was getting remarried. Anna was a foot taller than when he'd last seen her and now had a long plait down her back. She looked so excited and happy. Then he looked at Ella and Michael. She looked amazing. At that moment Michael pulled a face at the child who must be Sophie, who collapsed into giggles.

Over the years his mum had told him how the girls were getting on. In the beginning she'd even urged him to be a part of their lives, but she stopped doing that as soon as Michael came on the scene. He recognized a few of their old friends, but nobody noticed him as he walked by. He looked again at Tracy or was it Marlene, and was overwhelmed by the weirdest feeling; that he'd rather have been on the other side of the road.

Colour change

Theirs was a typical girls' bedroom with walls covered in posters of fantasy drawings. Clothes were hung from doors and draped over chairs. Make-up spilled from jars and pots and colourful jewellery decorated every surface.

'Shall we go to...' started Yasmin.
'the cinema?' said Yetta.
'I do wish you wouldn't...'
'do that. Sorry. I'll try not to,' said Yetta.

Yasmin pulled on her purple jumper and turned round to see her twin was wearing purple too.

'Oh, this is really a joke. I'll change,' said Yasmin raising her arms to pull the jumper off.

'But why bother? You know mother likes us to dress the same.'

'Well, it might've been okay when we were little, but we're older now and we should be different. We should be individual,' said Yasmin slipping on a black shirt.

'I don't know what all the fuss is about but hey, who cares?'

Picking up their bags they headed off to the cinema. On the way they passed the 'Cutting Edge' hairdressers. Yasmin, suddenly grabbed Yetta's arm and guided her into the shop. Yasmin explained to the receptionist that they would like some guidance from a hairdresser before they booked an appointment and they were asked to wait.

The hairdresser came and looked at them both and smiled. They were used to people smiling at their beautiful long blond hair and bright blue eyes. Yasmin took the lead.

'I want to look completely different from my twin, but we're still at school so I need a hairstyle that's not too outrageous.'

Yetta's face paled. 'But we've always looked the same. It'll be horrible to be a single rather than a pair.'

'Sorry Yetta. You'll always be my best friend, but we are different and I want to be me.'

'Well let me see how can I help you?' said the hairdresser. 'If you just wanted to be different you could have a bob. However, if you want something more dramatic, I could give you a very short wispy style. We could even add some low lights and then you could darken your make-up. Then again red hair always looks good.'

'I like the sound of wispy and low lights,' said Yasmin. 'Can you do it now?'

'Yes, we can fit you in. We're very quiet today. I'm Anna by the way.'

'Well, I don't like your hair ideas and I'm not wasting my afternoon. I'm off to the cinema. You coming?' said Yetta.

'No,' said Yasmin. 'I'll see you later.'

Yetta marched out of the shop and towards the cinema. She sat through the film on her own, taking in none of it. Usually, she sat with her twin. They rarely were apart and all the time she thought about how her sister would look with short, darker hair. She knew that when Yasmin went home their mother would explode with anger. There would be such a terrible row. Mother liked them looking like clones. She always said a pair was better than one, but really, she liked all the looks that came their way. Mother used them like ornaments. She would shout and scream and rant and rage at Yasmin for spoiling the image. Yetta began to be sorry that she'd walked out of Cutting Edge.

Yasmin felt very brave as her locks tumbled to the floor. Anna was funny and told her lots of amusing anecdotes as her hair was given low lights. She liked her new look, but wished Yetta had been sitting there with her. Usually, they were together and it felt odd being without her, although wasn't that partly what she wanted, to be an individual? It was later as she thought about going home that her confidence left her. Their mother was about to hit the roof and she was going to be shredded. In truth the pair of them never stood up to her. They let her bully them into being her 'pretty girls'. It was wrong but she was such a dominant woman. Instead of going home she went to sit on the swings in the park, but in the end, she knew she must go home.

Yasmin ran a hand through her short hair. This is what being an individual was about; standing up for things you believe. She opened the door and her mother was at her before she had time to think.

'What the hell have you done to your beautiful hair? Why you wicked, wicked girl.' The tirade went on, but although she tried to speak there was no space for her words. Then suddenly Yetta burst through the door and was standing beside her. Her hair was now shoulder length and had a gentle red tint to it. Their mother stopped and stared at Yetta.

'That Anna's very good, isn't she? I went after the cinema. I love your hair like that Yasmin. Do you like mine?'

'How dare you...?' their mother started.

'No mother! How dare you? You loved being the pretty blonde mum, with two identical cute blonde children. Now that we're older it isn't so good, but you like people stopping and staring. However, we need to find our own way now and not have you dictate how we should wear our hair or what subjects we take? We're seventeen and we're going to be individuals...,' said Yasmin.

'...and although we've lost our wow factor, we're going to start learning what it is like to make our own decisions.' said Yetta.

Their mother stood there, with mouth open wide, like a floundering goldfish.

'Why you ungrateful couple of...'

'Goodnight mother,' said both girls together as they linked arms and bounded upstairs.

After all, while it's great to explore being individuals, it was still good to be part of a pair.

Reunion

Alice really couldn't decide if she wanted to go or not. On the one hand it would be good to meet up with the twins. They'd been close friends at school, but that was forty years ago and they hadn't been in touch since. She knew that as identical twins they would have stayed close and been a huge part of each other's lives. It wasn't only their fault. She'd been busy. She'd raised two children and held down a job as a social worker. Most of the time she'd brought Sam and Sally up on her own after Derek left her for the love of his life. She'd thought that was her of course, but quickly discovered that when you meet the 'love of your life' that gives you carte blanche to be unfaithful, abandon your children and spend all your money on yourself and her. It didn't matter now. It was all a long time ago. At least the children were grown and happy.

'What would be the point of travelling all the way to London to see friends, who you now know nothing about? What would they talk about?' she thought. Perhaps she would just stay at home and do her garden. It would be less effort.

'Oh Mum,' said Sally, her eldest, 'go and enjoy yourself. Buy a new dress; pamper yourself. I love you to bits you know, but you're in danger of becoming a boring old fart. Get out there. It'll be great.'

'Where had her daughter learned such language?' she thought and then realized Sally was right. She was getting set in her ways. Somewhere along the way she'd grown frightened of doing anything new. She took a deep breath. She would go and make a weekend of it.

Alice met Rose and Lily in a surprisingly quiet pub near Charring Cross. She'd already booked into her hotel and unpacked her new dress, which she'd wear that evening. The hotel was one her daughter had stayed in and offered a variety of beauty treatments. She'd look through the brochure later and book some up for tomorrow. It felt strange to be away from her safe little environment, her comfortable home and beloved garden, but a little bit of her was excited too and she hadn't felt like that in years.

As soon as she saw Rose and Lily, she recognized them, which was surprising as they were now so different from each other. The long blonde hair of their youth was gone. Rose's hair was now white like a dove's feathers and Lily's was brown with sunshine streaks. Rose was neat in her pretty blouse and matching coloured cardigan, but Lily wore a striking patterned blouse and smart jacket. They all chatted and laughed as if they'd seen each other every day for the last forty years. There were no awkward silences and not once did Alice have to think about what to say. Soon she was telling them about her hotel and showing them the beauty treatment brochure. They all laughed at the idea of being wrapped in seaweed or massaged with what looked like mud.

'You were always up to things, Alice. I so admire you bringing up the children on your own. I thought it was hard enough with a husband,' said Rose.

Suddenly all her fears seemed silly. Rose and Lily had always been kind. Why would they have changed?

'Shall we join you at your hotel?' said Lily. 'It'd be such fun.'

'Oh yes, Alice, we've missed you. We were often wondering where you were and what you were doing,' said Rose.

Alice rummaged in her bag and brought out her phone and called the hotel. They had a vacant room.

Later she mused how the years had slipped away as soon as she'd met them again and how young she felt. She hadn't laughed so much in years. Thank heavens she'd had the courage to take a small step out of her comfort zone. She'd definitely do it again.

'I will not be sad that we've missed out forty years of each other's lives,' she thought, 'just glad we've met up again in time to enjoy ourselves.'

A Family Holiday

At my age life is simple. I love my family. Spending time with them is always a pleasure, but I also love my little home and tiny garden. I have roses growing over the door and a little bed of poppies intermixed with foxgloves. It's so pretty.

'Come on Mum,' said my dutiful son. 'We're off to Italy to a posh hotel, and you must come with us.'

'You're all right, 'I replied. 'I'd rather spend the summer at home. I've lots to do and I like the quiet. I haven't got the energy of you young things.'

'No Mum, the children really want you to be with us,' he insisted.

Well to cut a long story short, I ended up going. I packed my suitcase with care; a smart pull along, with light aluminum handles and a good sturdy base.

We weren't stopped at customs on leaving the U.K. I suppose they don't care what you take out; but when we arrived in Italy, the customs officers pulled over my son and his wife and rifled through all their possessions. I stood and watched, helplessly, comforting the children as best I could. I was glad they didn't go through my case though. Fancy having your smalls aired in public! My daughter-in-law's were tiny compared to mine. Eventually we were allowed to leave the airport but a few minutes later, the Carabinieri pulled over our hire car. Again, I waited on the sidelines while my son and his wife were questioned. It was quite an ordeal. The Italian police carry guns. It's not what we're used to.

When they were released, we travelled to the luxury hotel with a beautiful blue swimming pool.

'I'm so sorry, Mum. That was all rather frightening and this holiday was meant to be a treat for you,' said my son.

'Don't you worry, my boy,' I replied. 'It's not your fault. I know you'd never be involved in anything shady; not the way I brought you up. Now let's enjoy this holiday.'

The next morning, I was up really early, before any of the family. I grabbed my beach bag and went off towards the sea. The sun was low in the sky, just catching the water and it was a pleasantly cool day. There was only one other person on the beach and he was some way off. It was a young sailor, out for an early morning run. I know I shouldn't look, at my age, but he was fit, in both senses of the word. He was so quick, he relieved me of my bag, before I really noticed. When I looked after him, I saw that he'd dropped an envelope on the beach. I became a little flustered. Here was I, on my own, on a beach, in a strange land and had just had an encounter with a handsome young reprobate. I must have walked further along the beach than I thought, because, on the way back, I couldn't find the right road. The sun was getting hot and my family would be worrying where I was. I tried to call them, but bless my cotton socks, my phone had run out of charge. I was always forgetting to charge the stupid thing.

Eventually I found myself in a little town and took a taxi. Luckily, the driver knew the hotel and drove me back there in no time at all. Just as well I'd kept my money in my belt bag.

I didn't mention my encounter on the beach, or getting lost, to my son. There was no point in worrying him any more than he was already.

'If you want to go for a little walk tomorrow, Mum, just knock on our door. I'll come with you. Anything might happen if you wander off on your own, and you don't even speak the language.'

'Oui, je fait,' I replied.

'I'm not sure if that's even right, but it's French, Mum, not Italian.'

'Oh, so it is. You mustn't worry about me, my boy. I'm fine and what will be, will be,' I said with a smile.

I caught him raising his eyebrows at his wife, but decided to let it pass. No point in starting a row.

The rest of the holiday was wonderful, with lots of swimming, laughter and fun. I even managed a trip into the nearest town to visit the bank and sort out my foreign cash. And we all went on a noisy and exhausting day trip to the mountains.

After the holiday was over, I stopped off at my son's house for the night. As soon as they went to bed, I went online and checked my bank balance. It had certainly been a good idea to sell the opium and digitalis from last year's flowers, to that fit young Italian sailor.

Now I can go home to peace and quiet; tend to my beautiful garden and think about next year. There are some advantages to getting older. Nobody thinks you could be selling drug ingredients on the quiet!

I remember, I remember

Three things happened when I was seven years old. It was a chance remark from my sister that brought back those memories.

We were talking about a child who'd gone missing from a village near where we lived.

'Whenever a child goes missing, I always think of Sandra,' Katy said.

'Sandra who?' I asked.

'You know Sandra, from your class, who went missing. If I remember, surely you do?'

All the memories came flooding back to when I was seven. They started with the Autumn of 1959. Back then I used to make myself some breakfast and take myself off for the day. Nowadays you'd accuse a parent of being neglectful, but in those days, it was perfectly acceptable for children to be out playing and exploring on their own.

Now it so happened that both my parents were strict atheists, but my aunt and grandparents were devout Christians. I liked the idea of Christianity; of being a member of a group and having a God to call on when you'd got yourself into a mess. I used to go to church on my own and was always made welcome. Then various friends said come along with my family. One of them was Sandra Weston.

'Meet me outside the church at nine fifteen and we'll go and find a seat together,' she said.

Now Sandra and I were friendly but we were by no means best friends. She was nice enough with a tendency to copy others, but I thought it would be good to try out a new church with a family. I'd been to a Catholic church, a Church of England one, a Methodist one and a Baptist one. I'm not pretending that I understood any of the differences between the church disciplines. I can still see the Church, but I can't remember which denomination it was.

I remember dressing carefully for Church; wearing socks without any holes, a plain skirt and a neat cardigan and I skipped happily along the mile or so of pavement until I came to the church in Oxford Lane. It was a quiet morning, but when I arrived there was literally no-one there. Had Sandra tricked me? I peeked my head around the church door and the vicar saw me.

'Why hello there. You're early. Did you remember to put your clock backward an hour?' he asked.

My face must have fallen. 'Oh, don't worry about it my dear,' he said. 'Come on in,' and in I went. It was dark in the church compared to the bright daylight outside.

'I'll just finish putting out these hymn books and then I'll take you through to the back and make you some orange juice,' he smiled.

I really can't explain why, but I suddenly thought I don't want to be here with this creepy man. I shuddered inside with fear. You know the saying, *the hair stood up on the back of my neck,* well I think it really did.

'No thanks,' I called. 'I'll go and meet my friend and come back later.' I was out of that church so quickly. I don't know at what point I started running, but I found myself running all the way home. My parents were totally unimpressed by my little adventure.

'I do wish you didn't have such an overactive imagination,' said mother.

At school on Monday, Sandra asked me why I hadn't turned up and I made up some excuse. Later I came to regret not meeting her that week and the next Sunday I overslept.

A week later she didn't come to school. I asked the teacher if she was ill and was told to go and sit down and not ask questions. After two weeks, I asked my mother.

'Has Sandra moved? She doesn't come to school any more or is she on some wonderful holiday?' I remember that mother didn't look me in the eyes as she told me to go away and lay the table.

The following week I was in bed, diagnosed with glandular fever. I was there forever or that's what it felt like.

'If you're ill enough to be off school, you stay in bed,' mother said. Of course, I didn't stay in bed and I didn't want to be at home any more than she wanted me there. At the back of my mind, I suppose I assumed that Sandra must have been off school with glandular fever, but I hardly ever thought of her again.

Now here was my sister telling me that she'd gone missing. I did some research and discovered that she'd never been found and then I remembered the creepy vicar. As a child I believed my parents when they kept on telling me I had an over large imagination, but as an adult I believe that if we take an instant fear of someone there is usually a reason. I dressed myself smartly and took myself down to the local cop shop and asked if anyone was still looking into the case of Sandra Weston.

I was called into an interview room by Detective Inspector Chester. He listened quietly to my story about my strong fear of the vicar, made a few notes, thanked me for my help and bade me good-bye.

He probably thought I was bonkers. Fancy telling a policeman that you had a bad feeling about someone when you were a child. He was right. I must put it behind me.

Three months later there was a ring on my doorbell and there was Inspector Chester. I invited him in and made him tea.

'I looked into the background of Reverend Alan Wilson. There were quite a few outstanding complaints about him and he left the church suddenly and emigrated to Australia, so I notified the authorities over there of our interest in him.'

'I thought you must've thought I was mad coming to see you,' I blurted out.

'Indeed no. Then I thought what if he'd tried to abuse Miss Weston and she'd struggled? What if it had all gone wrong and he'd killed her? What would he have done with her body, so I went and looked at the burial records for the church in Oxford Lane. I found there was one more grave than there was on the records.'

My blood ran cold. I knew what he was about to say.

'I'm sorry to tell you that we exhumed the body from that grave and it was that of a child. We're checking her dental records to see if it's Sandra Weston, but almost certainly it is.'

'Will Reverend Wilson be arrested in Australia?' I asked.

'He was taken in for questioning and put in a cell overnight. In the morning he was found dead in his cell. I don't have the full details. You might be disappointed that he was never brought to trial or paid for his crime, but I'd like you to remember that because of you, Sandra's parents have finally got closure and can grieve properly.'

I thanked Inspector Chester for listening to me and for all his hard work on the case.

Rest in Peace Sandra. I'm sorry I wasn't a better friend.

Searching

Tia knew she had to look. She had to know who she was and where she'd come from. The hardest part would be explaining this to Mum and Dad. They were the best parents you could ever ask for, but she still needed to know what her biological parents looked like; what they did for a living and of course the big question, why they didn't want to bring her up.

That evening Tia and her family settled down to eat. Dad had made one of his wonderful curries, not like the ones from the shop. This was mild enough so that you could taste all the flavours, but hot enough to give a bit of a kick. The smell of spices wafted through the room.

'Mum, Dad, you know I love you both, don't you?'

'Yes of course we do,' said Mum.

'Well nothing I do is ever going to change how I feel about you,' Tia said.

Mum and Dad exchanged wary glances.

'It's just that when I turn eighteen next month, I intend to look for my biological parents. I know you're not keen. I've tried to talk about it to you before, but I just want to see where I come from, that's all.'

'Oh my God,' said Mum and rushed out of the room.

Dad's face crumpled in front of her. His eyes grew wide and his face thinned. There was silence. She realized for the first time he looked his age. She noticed the wrinkles and mottled skin. He placed his fork down on the plate and drank his entire glass of wine down with one gulp.

'Dad, I'm so sorry. I didn't think you'd be happy about it, but I had no idea it would have this effect on you.'

'Of course you didn't Tia. Why would you? We've pretended to ourselves, all these years, that we'd never have to tell you.'

Tia picked up her own wine and took a sip. She felt like she was waiting for results from tests for a life-threatening illness. Dad's face was serious. She waited quietly while he gathered his thoughts.

'Your mum and I met later on in life. I was forty eight and Mum was forty one. As you know we discovered we couldn't have children, so we applied to adopt.'

'Yes, I know Dad and I'm so glad you did.'

'We jumped through all sorts of hoops. There were medicals, our house was visited by the adoption agency lady, my income was examined.'

'I do understand how hard it must've been, Dad, honestly.'

'Oh my darling girl, I don't know how to tell you, so I'm going to come straight out with it.' He paused. 'We failed. They said we were too old. They said we could never have a baby.'

'But I don't understand,' said Tia.

'Your mother, as you can imagine, was distraught, and then by some miracle, a friend of mine told us about a newborn baby in the local children's home. She was being physically looked after, but nobody gave her any love. She was left to cry in a room on her own for hours. It upset him and there was us, desperate for a baby with all the love in the world to give.'

'What are you telling me, Dad?'

'She was you. My friend smuggled you out one night and brought you to us. I forged adoption papers and we moved away, gave up all our friends and contacts and started a new life. Not even the man who helped us knew where we went. So, you see as soon as you start your enquiries we'll be found out.'

'I just don't understand. You abducted me? I can't believe that you and Mum would do such a thing. I can't get my head round this.'

'Of course, we knew it was wrong in our hearts, but we justified it to ourselves. You were being ignored in the children's home, not nurtured. The staff hadn't time for you. They didn't care. Believe me you can justify anything if you try hard enough.'

'But how come your friend wasn't stopped? He couldn't just walk out with a baby.'

'Well things weren't like they are today. There was no CCTV on the doors. He literally wrapped you in a blanket and waited until the coast was clear. You weren't missed until morning.'

'Did your friend get caught?'

'No, he wasn't seen and he went back to work as normal the following morning. The enquiry concluded that they should keep all the doors locked in future. They thought someone had walked in off the streets and snatched you.'

Tia couldn't think of anything else to say. Her parents were such quiet, ordinary people. How could she believe that she was a stolen child? She ran out of the room. Her mind was buzzing with so many thoughts and questions. Eventually she fell asleep, fully clothed.

In the morning she went downstairs to find her mum and dad waiting for her in the kitchen. They were drinking strong coffee, steaming hot. Somehow Tia found it reassuring to see them sitting at the large oak table, in their dressing gowns, hugging mugs of coffee.

'Are you going to go ahead and try and find your original family?' asked Dad. Tia entered the beamed room with white-washed walls. She could hear a thrush singing through the open window. Its song told of the joy of life, which was in complete contrast to how Tia was feeling.

'Of course not,' said Tia. 'How can I? You'd both be in trouble with the police, but I have to admit I'm sad that I'll never know anything about them.'

Her mum went out of the kitchen and came back with a box. She placed it on the table.

'There's not much we know, but maybe it's something.'

Tia opened the lid carefully. There was a terry toweling nappy, plastic pants and a yellow Babygro suit. A tiny hospital label lay at the bottom of the box, with the name Baby Evans and a fragile faded newspaper cutting lay under a tiny pink machine knitted cardigan. She picked up the cutting, which told of a baby going missing from a local authority children's home in East Sussex.

'Thanks Mum and Dad, I'd like to keep these.' When they nodded, she squirrelled the box away up to her bedroom. On re-entering the kitchen, she said, 'Let's plan the party for my eighteenth then.'

She watched her parents visibly relax. Plans were made for the local village hall to be hired and live music was booked.

But Tia still wanted to know about her biological parents. Much as she loved her parents and would protect them, she decided she would make every effort to search for her biological parents, even if she could never introduce herself. Instead of going to school the following Monday, she went to the local library, where they kept large heavy books of old newspapers. She asked for the newspapers for the year 1968. They brought her the Times and the Daily Mail. Settled in a quiet corner of the high windowed library, she searched for information about a stolen baby. She found reading these papers nearly twenty years old was interesting in its own right, but she kept her focus, scanning and skimming the pages. It was just before lunchtime when she found what she'd been looking for. The article was headed 'Baby Stolen at Dead of Night'. A baby was abducted from Fairbourne Children's Home in the middle of the night. Baby Evans was the daughter of convicted murderers Bessie and Charlie Evans, who had killed their neighbours, George and Amy Dobbs, after a row about their loud music. The murders had taken place six months earlier when Bessie and Charlie Evans, high on drugs, had broken into the Dobb's house around midnight and stabbed them. It is thought that Amy died immediately but there were signs that George took some time to die. Clear fingerprints of Mr and Mrs Evans were found both at the scene and on the knives. Mrs Evans had her baby in prison, one week after being sentenced to life. She called her baby, Charlotte. It is expected that Bessie and Charlie Evans will serve a minimum of twenty years.

Tia was devastated. She'd thought her parents might be disappointing, perhaps an unmarried mum, even someone sent to prison, but double murderers! In her most imaginative of dreams, she'd never concocted that end to her search.

She looked closely at the yellowing printed pictures of her biological parents. There was a slight family resemblance, but nothing more. Then a thought struck her. Nobody knew who she really was. Being abducted meant that she would never have to be burdened by the Evan's wickedness. She wouldn't think of them as her parents. Tia looked around the library. No-one was watching. She'd burn the pages. With heart pounding she tore the pages from the binding and stuffed them into her school bag.

The Woman Who Didn't Smile

I was sitting in the cafe finishing my coffee, when I noticed a very old man with a beautiful smile lead in an old lady, who was as fragile as a little bird. Her skin was brown and crinkled like screwed up wrapping paper. There was no light in her eyes and her face was dour, but the man smiled at everybody as they wove their way through a jumble of tables and chairs. He tried to help her sit down on a padded bench against the wall, and she argued with him that she couldn't get her feet under the table and that there wasn't enough space. Gently he moved the table and escorted her around the side of it. When she'd sat down, he sat with her, talking softly and calming her. Five minutes later he got up to go to the counter and get their drinks.

'I won't be long,' he said. 'And you can see where I'm going.'

The queue meandered back towards the door, but the man waved at her as he stood sideways making sure she was always in view.

Slowly I sipped my cooling coffee and nodded to my companion, who was on her phone. I liked watching people and although the cafe was crowded, nobody seemed to rush us.

The tiny little bird woman tried to engage the man sitting near her in conversation, but he stoically resisted, concentrating on his partner. She tapped him on the shoulder and pointed to something on the floor.

'You've dropped that,' she said.

It was a dirty serviette, which probably wasn't his in the first place, but he relented and bent down and picked it up.

'Thank you,' he said.

A few minutes later the little bird woman became agitated. 'Where's he gone? Where's he gone?' she repeated parrot like.

One of the waitresses, who was cleaning the tables, stopped and sat by her.

'Look there he is,' she said pointing to the counter. 'He's waving to you. He'll be back in a minute. Can you see him?'

The tiny bird woman calmed down again and soon the old man wove his way back through the tables and chairs, carrying a tray with two drinks and a cake. He sat down beside her, helping her with her drink and cake, talking to her in his lovely gentle voice. All the time he was smiling at her and anyone else who looked over to the table. But her eyes remained dull and no smile lit her face.

I felt sad for the man that he worked so hard for no response, but there was nothing I could do. My companion offered me another coffee but I was happy just sitting in the warmth of the cafe.

When I looked over to the table again, they had finished their coffee and cake and he was still talking to her gently. Suddenly she looked at him and patted his hand. He closed his eyes as if to treasure the moment and I realized that I'd seen something special.

'Come on, it's time to go, Mum. We need to get your coat on,' I heard my companion say. I stood up to get the coat off the back of my chair and caught my face in the mirror behind me. I was shocked that my face held no smile. I was smiling inside but my face, looked vacant, almost cross.

I turned to my companion. I couldn't remember her name, but she'd call me Mum.

I patted her arm and said, 'You're a good girl. Thanks for bringing me here. I do enjoy it,' and I saw a smile light up her face; a warm smile, full of love.

I hope she could see I was smiling too.

The Plan

I slipped the phone into my bag, without Tracy noticing. I didn't want to steal from Tracy. She was my best friend, but I needed the phone for my plan to work.

When I got back from school Mum was busy cooking. She said hello, but was focusing on preparing the meal. Everything had to be perfect for when Max came home. Although I was hungry, I kept quiet. I didn't want to make her life harder and one of the rules was, we had to eat as a family.

I kept going over my plan, in my head. It had to work.

In the end I didn't have to wait long. Max came home in a foul mood. We sat down at the dining room table and I didn't look at him, while Mum served the meal. It was best not to say anything when he was scowling because he would turn on you. I knew to keep absolutely quiet, like I wasn't there. Mum brought in a wonderful meal and although I was only allowed a small plate, I couldn't wait to eat it. He pushed the food round for a minute, scowled and then swiped the plate onto the floor. I knew what would come next. We all did.

At first when Max arrived on the scene, I thought he was fun. He bought us presents and played games. My mum always had flowers. He was so attentive and kind, but gradually the little rules crept in. Soon my friends weren't welcome round our house and I wasn't allowed to stay up late, not even on holidays. Next reading in bed was banned and breaking the rules had consequences. Once, I had to miss school for a week because the bruises were so bad.

The saddest thing though was my mother never stood up for me. Although I'm at secondary school, I'm tiny. My dad says I'm like a bag of bones, but I don't see him much. To be fair to Mum, her beatings were far more severe than mine and happened more often, but I would've liked her to say, 'Stop that!' just once. Then I'd know she still loved me. It never happened.

'The carrots are bloody cold, woman,' Max screamed. 'Can't you even cook a decent meal? I'm out all day...'

I rushed out of the room and grabbed the phone. I switched on the video and filmed through a crack in the door, my mum being battered to a pulp. I was totally choked up seeing what was happening, but decided as I couldn't fight him, I'd have to do something else to change our lives.

I ran to the bathroom and locked the door. It was the safest room in the house. First, I called the police and then I Facebooked, tweeted and emailed all the contacts on Tracy's phone. It didn't take long. I was surprised how clear the video was. He hadn't noticed I was missing yet. Mum had stopped crying, but she was still alive. She was making small whimpering sounds, but I could still hear thuds and plates breaking. I was not coming out of the bathroom until he stormed out of the house. Seeing me would only set him off again, with a new surge of anger.

This time though the carnage was stopped when the police arrived. They took Max away and Mum was sent to hospital. I liked the power of having a phone. Mrs Hardy from next door said she'd look after me until Dad arrived, but she didn't want to really, so I told her I'd be fine on my own, and I am. I'm eating Max's chocolate biscuits now. I've bagged up all of his belongings and stuck them by the bins. Tomorrow I'll use the money I found in his wardrobe to change the locks.

I've just got to hope Tracy will forgive me, when I return her phone. I'm sure she will. She's the one who taught me how to use social media.

For now, I'll just finish burning the last of Max's photos. The warmth from the flame is strangely comforting and I like watching them curl and melt in the bin. By the time Mum gets back there won't be a trace of him, but maybe we should move, just in case they let him out.

See how you run

The shrill of the fire alarm pierced the air. On and on it went. This was obviously not a test. Robert swore. He should've gone to the office today. Now Julia would get her wish to become a partner in the firm. She was a good lawyer, but nothing special. Oh well there was nothing he could do about it. He'd heard the thundering footsteps past his flat, but there was no way he was going to make it down forty-two flights of stairs and the lift would be out of order. He'd text his friends to alert them that he was still in the flat and shut all the doors and windows. Maybe he'd be lucky.

Out of the corner of his eyes he caught a movement under his desk. He slid his chair backwards to take a look.

'Well, I never. Mice! Three of them,' he thought. 'How on earth did they get there?' Then he laughed out loud. 'I wonder if they're blind and where's the farmer's wife?'

Still the alarm pulsed its dreadful warning, but a knock on the door heralded the entrance of Mrs Thorn. She came bustling in, carrying two mugs of tea.

'Good morning, Robert. I'd just made a brew, when the alarm went and I had a feeling you might not be joining the hoards running down the stairs.

'Come on in, Mrs Thorn.'

'Are you all right dear? How are you feeling?' she said.

Robert smiled inwardly. Mrs T was still a nurse. She may have retired more than twenty years ago but it was in her blood. She just couldn't help being a caring old soul.

'I'm fine. Wouldn't have chosen to die in a fire but there's nothing I can do, nor you, I guess. Hey I've got three blind mice running round my flat. Are you the farmer's wife? Have you got the knife?

'What are you talking about, dear? How do you know the mice are blind? They didn't used to be.'

'It was a joke,' said Robert. 'What do you mean, didn't used to be?'

'Oh nothing.'

'Well time's precious, but what do you want to talk about?' He liked the old girl. She was always so kind.

'Ah I know, I'll tell you about my plumber. I had a dripping tap,' said Mrs Thorn. 'So, I called out a plumber. He seemed such a nice young man, just like you. Do you know how much he was going to charge me?'

'No,' said Robert. It was just his luck to end his days chatting to an old girl about plumbing.

'Well, he said he'd do it for £600, but as it was me, he'd only charge £500! £500 I ask you, for a dripping tap.'

'That's a bit steep,' said Robert.

'Yes, that's what I thought,' said Mrs Thorn. 'Those mice you were talking about were mine you know. I wanted a dog, but we weren't allowed to have one in these flats, so I bought some mice. They make great pets. When I heard the alarm go, I let them out. I may not be able to get downstairs, but I thought I'd give them a chance.'

The morning was turning out to be surreal or just plain mad.

'I wanted to say how much I appreciated your help with my shopping, when you first moved in,' said Mrs Thorn.

'You were very welcome. I'm sorry I couldn't continue. Did the internet shopping I set up work out okay?'

'Well, they bring my shopping each week, but they moan so much about having to bring it up on the lift. Moaning old so and so's. Just like the plumber when I said I was going to pay him £50, which I thought was a fair price.'

'I bet he didn't like that much. Still, he was being greedy. I wonder if he got out.'

'Oh no. He argued with me and so I agreed to pay the £500 and when he bent over, I clocked him one with the coffee pot.'

'Is he O.K.?'

'No of course he isn't. That's why I had to start the fire. To get rid of the body.'

There was a mad look in her eyes. What could Robert do? He had completely misjudged her.

'I knew you wouldn't be able to get out, but you could've come and spent some time with me since your accident. You're selfish too.'

'Mrs Thorn, just because I'm in a wheelchair, doesn't mean I've stopped working. I have less time than I used to. It takes me longer to everything.'

'Well, it doesn't matter now, does it? Drink your tea.'

'I will, thank you. I'll just get some sugar.'

'I'll get it for you,' she said as she stood up and headed for the kitchen.

As soon as she turned her back, Robert grabbed his phone and texted a group message to his friends and colleagues.

FIRE NEXT DOOR. STUCK IN FLAT WITH MAD NEIGHBOUR. HELP.

Hopefully one of them would get help.

'Sugar,' said Mrs Thorn and she made herself comfy on the chair next to his.

The Following Day

Emma's ankle throbbed painfully and her head hurt. She lay back on the bed, surrounded by faded green curtains. The smell of disinfectant reminded her where she was. 'What a waste of time!' she thought. If only she hadn't popped out this morning to buy some nibbles for the drive home. She consciously switched off from her surroundings. It wasn't difficult. An image of Scott came into her mind and she could feel heat rush to her cheeks.

'How could she have spent the night with a complete stranger?' Somehow, she'd just known that they'd be good together. He smelt so male, but fresh like the sea. Still dressed in her navy business suit, she'd slipped into the bar for a quick drink before dinner. The room was modern, but without any personality and dimly lit. He'd looked over immediately she walked into the room and she became aware of his eyes following her. Once she'd collected a large glass of chilled chardonnay from bar, she paused and looked for a quiet place to sit.

'There's space at this table,' he said standing up. 'It's horrible coming to these places on your own, isn't it?'

She'd almost been hypnotized by those brown eyes. She remembered thinking that he wasn't put off by her mass of copper curls or that she wasn't wearing sexy high heels, which seemed to be mandatory these days. It was a shame she wouldn't see him again. They'd both been very clear that the night was a one-off, no strings, break from reality. Her hand went to her face, where he'd stroked her so gently the night before. It felt wet and she realized she was bleeding.

It was a good job he wasn't here now. He wouldn't want to take her to bed if he could see her bruised face and torn trousers. She looked as if she'd gone ten rounds with a boxer. She smiled faintly thinking about how her mugger hadn't managed to steal her bag. Probably she shouldn't have fought back, but it was easy to be wise after the event. It wasn't even a designer bag but it contained her phone, which was also her diary, address book, music player and media contact device. She hadn't backed it up for ages but she would do as soon as she got out of this place. Her reactions had been instinctive. The guy had tried to pull the bag from her shoulder as he'd passed. She'd pulled back. He'd punched her and she'd kicked him as hard as she could. This gave her the few seconds she needed to get away. Then she'd run and fallen grazing her hands and hurting her head. Luckily several passers-by gathered round her so her mugger, standing a few feet away, shrugged and went off.

It was such a pain to be stuck here and the police wanted her to go in and look at some pictures later. The fact that he'd hit her meant they were taking the mugging seriously, which was all very well, but it would eat up her time. She didn't want to think about it.

Scott's dark head came back into her thoughts again. She remembered him kissing her, the warmth of his mouth, his tentative questioning and their later passion. She could feel herself being aroused, just by the thought of his lean, firm body. Oh, if only she could see him again, but she was just visiting Cheltenham for a tedious conference and he lived here; staying at the hotel while his house was being decorated. Perhaps she was remembering him as better than he actually was, to justify her rash behaviour. She didn't usually do the one-night stand scene. It was far too risky and you always regretted it the following day. She realized though that she didn't regret one moment.

She closed her eyes to indulge in a minute's fantasy, while she waited to be seen by the casualty doctor. The clanking of the curtain being drawn, at the foot of her bed, brought her back to reality.

And there he was standing before her with a surprised look on his face. He smiled. A big, warm, happy smile that made crinkly lines appear around his eyes. 'So, he's a doctor,' she thought and she knew in that moment there would be other nights.

Single

Della gulped down her too hot coffee as she made her way to the front door. Shoving her feet in high heeled shoes, she grabbed her coat and slammed the door. Every morning was the same. There was no-one about as she speeded off towards Bigwood Station. She could hear the train coming as she pulled into the car park.

Diving through the doors she headed for the only empty seat. It was an aisle seat so she knew she needed to get her make-up on quickly as the train would fill up at the next stop. With an expertise, that she didn't appreciate, she shadowed and lined her eyes and added black mascara. She glossed her lips in a subtle shade of pink and with a few flicks of her comb her hair fell into its neat bob. Other passengers watched fascinated at the transformation.

By the next station Della was sitting with one elegant leg crossed over the other and was calmly reading her book. The doors opened and passengers piled in. One lady leaned over Della's seat. Della gave her a cool look and then sneezed loudly in her direction. The lady shuffled away. A hint of a smile hovered on Della's lips. She was, after all, an experienced commuter.

Alice poured herself another cup of freshly brewed coffee and sat down at the kitchen table with The Times. Absentmindedly she stroked Albert, her Scottish terrier. She waited until the coffee was lukewarm before finishing it and then padded upstairs to the shower.

Although it was a bright day, there was a chill in the air, so Alice slipped on a cashmere jumper over her blouse. She took time and care putting on her make-up in the special magnifying mirror that her daughter had bought her for Christmas. She applied a thin eyeliner to her eyelids and then a layer of mascara to her lashes.

'Not too bad,' she thought to herself as she checked the mirror one last time. Pulling on sensible flat boots she slipped a lead on Albert and left the house.

Arriving at the club, she settled Albert in the corner of the room and went to join her friends at the bar. Mary Entwhistle carried Alice's drink back to the table for her and made a fuss of Albert. Soon a number of other women joined them. Alice knew she was lucky to be part of the Bigwood Ladies group and settled back to hear all their latest news. Nobody mentioned that her lipstick was too wide for her mouth, her eyes were smudged with thick liner or that she was wearing one brown and one blue boot.

Della arrived at the office calm and relaxed having finished another chapter of the novel she was reading. Before she hung up her coat Mr Arnold said he wanted to see her. She raised an eyebrow, but followed him out of the room.

Without preamble he said, 'We want to offer you the position of junior partner, here at Arnold and Griffith. Initially you'll take over two of my high-profile cases, but in the longer term, you'll become a senior partner and I'll retire. What d'you say Della?'

She took a deep breath and held out her hand. 'I'm delighted to accept,' she said.

Inside she wanted to jump up and down and scream. This was what she'd been working towards for five years. Now her mum would be proud of her. In fact, she'd pop in on the way home tonight.

Alice walked back from the club with Albert, stopping to chat with people along the way. The sun warmed her face. Still there was the rest of the afternoon and evening to get through on her own, so she decided to buy herself a little treat. Popping into the corner shop she picked up a bottle of sherry and three packets of jammy dodgers. She liked these biscuits and so did Albert.

When she got home she couldn't be bothered to cook. She'd had a proper meal at lunch time so she opened the sherry and the biscuits and settled down to watch Floggit. That Paul Martin was such a nice man. As the sun went down so did the biscuits.

Then she heard a key in the lock. It could only be one person.

'Hello Mum,' said Della. 'Oh my goodness, what are you doing? Drinking in the afternoon and there's crumbs everywhere.'

'Hello Della dear. It's good to see you,' Alice smiled.

'Have you had your evening meal yet? Don't tell me you're not eating properly and living on biscuits. You'll have to go in a home if you can't look after yourself.'

'Sit down Della. I've been out with my club today and had a proper meal and I'll go into a home if and when I want to.'

'Sorry Mum. I worry about you.'

'When it suits you, but in the weeks in between I get on with my life. Now can I get you something?'

Della sat down and brushed some crumbs from the chair.

'I wish you wouldn't let that dog sit on the chairs and if you stopped feeding him biscuits there wouldn't be crumbs everywhere.'

'That's true, but I don't mind if Albert makes a few crumbs. Now have you just come round to nag me?'

Della paused and then smiled, 'I've been made a junior partner, Mum. Isn't that fantastic? Not many women my age are made partners.'

'That's very nice dear. I'm glad you're pleased.' Alice stroked Albert's ears. 'Poor girl,' she thought, 'on her own at thirty-five. There's enough time to be on your own at seventy two.' She poured herself another sherry and caught a look of disappointment on Della's face.

Raising her glass she said, 'Well done Della. I'm very proud of you.'

'Are you Mum? You don't look it.'

'Of course I am; it's just that I worry about you too.'

'Me? Why on earth would you worry about me? I'm young, fit and healthy and have a well-paid job.'

'You never seem to have time to savour the good things in life. When did you last have a day off?'

'Mum, you don't understand. I'm in a very competitive business. I have to be sharp and keep working to stay ahead. I'm achieving more than most. Can't you be proud?'

'I *am* proud, but just remember you're not that young and time's marching if you're planning to do the married and baby thing.'

'Oh mother! I'm off home. Early start tomorrow.' She paused by the door and looked back. Her mother was ferreting in a drawer.

'Here, Della. Take this. It's your father's ring. He would have been so proud of you becoming a partner.'

Della looked at the ring. Yes he would've understood. How she missed him. She smiled and hugged her mother.

'Thanks Mum.'

As Della was drifting off to sleep that night, wearing her father's ring, she remembered that however busy he was at work, he always took Sunday completely off. They used to go out as a family to parks, forests, lakes and in the winter to the museums. She couldn't remember when she'd last taken a whole day off from work. At week-ends she caught up on reading cases and made notes.

When she got to work that morning, she phoned her mum.

'Let's spend Sunday together and go to Bluebell Lake. I'll pick you up at nine.'

'That would be lovely,' Alice said. 'Make that eleven.' I'll look forward to it.'

For a moment Della felt really cross. Half the day would be gone before they got there, but then she realized her mum was right. She really didn't know how to relax properly anymore.

'Eleven is fine,' she said to her mum.

'See you then,' said Alice, putting the phone down and rolling over to go back to sleep. After all it was only eight thirty!

Curtain Crescent

Of all the residents of Curtain Crescent, it was Mrs Lake who didn't quite fit in. In this highly competitive cul-de-sac, her husband was by far the richest but as Mrs Lake knew, being wealthy didn't bring happiness. It allowed him the privilege of trading her in for a younger model. The girl, Tracy Beeston, could have been their daughter, if they'd been able to have children. She sighed. There was no point in being bitter. He had signed over their lovely home to her and paid her a reasonable allowance. She knew she could've sued him for more, but what was the point? At least this way their relationship had remained civil.

Her neighbours were all trying to show that they were better off than each other, but she'd opted out of all that. They still invited her along to gatherings, especially if they wanted her to cook. She was an excellent cook. She spent her days trying new recipes or baking for small events. It gave her a small income but also a sense that she was still a worthwhile human being.

Every now and again, unknown to the others, she'd popped round to Emily Cardigan's house with a few cakes, or a special soup. She'd felt sorry for the poor old girl. It had been a shock to them all when Emily had died and found to have been dead for a fortnight without anyone noticing. They were all bad neighbours, herself included.

Today, she'd received two letters; both from Emily's solicitors, Messrs Baker and McKay. The first was inviting her and her neighbours to their offices to pick a piece of Emily's jewellery. How kind a person had Emily had been, to be giving her jewels to such self-centred people.

The second letter contained a small journal that Emily had written. She would read that later, after the meeting with the neighbours.

The next day they were all shown into Mr Baker's meeting room by Zelda, his P.A. She encouraged them to take seats at the long table. The jewellery was placed in the middle of the table.

Mr Baker swept into the room and seated himself.

'Ladies, before we come to the matter of distributing these beautiful items, I'm sorry to say that the blue diamond, an extremely rare gem, is missing. It was designated to be auctioned to build a children's playground. Does anyone know of its whereabouts?'

'What exactly are you suggesting? That one of us has stolen it?' said Mrs Hill. Her voice was extremely sharp and everyone in the room shrunk just a little bit.

'Indeed not,' said Mr Baker, 'but one of you could've gone in to tidy up and put it somewhere safe.'

'I'm not sure why we need a children's playground anyway,' said Mrs Aston. Mrs Lake hasn't even got any children and mine and Mrs Hill are grown up. Mrs Pike and Mrs Henry's children have passes to the leisure centre, so they have access to a swimming pool, gym, tennis courts and all those other things young people do.'

'And where on earth was this playground going to be sited?' asked Mrs Pike. There's no spare land for miles around.'

'Miss Cardigan's idea was that her house should be pulled down. It was badly in need of repair anyway and the play park would be built there,' said Mr Baker.

'Well thank goodness the blue diamond has disappeared. You'd have dog walkers and druggies congregating in our little crescent. It would devalue our properties,' said Mrs Henry.

Mr Baker raised his eyes to the ceiling. *What a bunch of awful women*, he thought.

'Mrs Lake, you haven't said anything. What are your thoughts on the playground?'

'Oh, I don't know. I've still got a Victoria sponge and trifle to make for a funeral I'm catering for.'

Mr Baker gave up, 'Well if nobody knows where the blue diamond is, we'd better decide which piece of jewellery…'

But he didn't get to finish the sentence, as the ladies of Curtain Crescent all leaned forward and grabbed a piece. Mrs Lake, a little slow on the uptake, realized that the only piece left, was a blue heart made of sapphires and seed pearls.

'Right, well that's sorted,' said Mr Baker. 'Please tell Zelda which piece you have taken, on the way out, for our records,' and he snapped shut his file and left the room.

'Well girls,' said Mrs Hill, 'back to mine for tea?'

'Thank you, but I must get on with my baking,' said Mrs Lake and left the room.

When she'd gone, Mrs Aston asked, 'Whose funeral is she baking for?'

'No idea,' said Mrs Henry.

Mrs Lake kicked off her shoes as soon as she got home and slipped on her comfy slippers. She settled down on the sofa with Emily's journal.

She could hear Emily's voice speaking as she read her words.

I was once a famous ballerina. My name was Emelia Blueheart. Being the top of my profession, I became much admired and men bought me the most beautiful jewels, hoping that they would marry me and share my fortune. As is always the way, I fell head over heels in love. He was a young actor called Michael Montfort. We married and I had three months of absolute bliss. Then I had a fall and broke my foot. Afterwards I could never dance again. Michael realized that I was no longer the money-making machine he'd hoped for. Luckily for me, although I didn't realize it at the time, much of my money was in Switzerland and so I've had enough to live comfortably; and I kept all my jewels and enjoyed looking at them over the years. My favourite is a little blue heart made of sapphires and seed pearls. Michael gave that to me.

For several years I settled for my life and then one day I saw Michael on the television. He was planning to marry a girl half his age and he was quoted as saying she was the love of his life.

I cannot begin to express my sadness and anger; my feelings of utter desolation and despair. I found out the next day that his fiancé was Catherine Lily, the famous actress. You will know that she died in a car crash, but what you won't know was that I arranged it. If I could never be happy, I didn't see why Michael should be. I spoke to a contact I had when I lived in London and he sabotaged the car. The price he asked for the deed was the blue diamond.

Did I ever regret my actions, you will ask? No, not really. I was sorry for Catherine Lily of course, but Michael deserved all the pain I'd arranged for him.

You may be asking why I put the blue diamond in my will, when I didn't own it anymore. I just thought it would make the witches of Curtain Crescent be worried, at least for a while. I wish I could've been there to see their faces. Mrs Lake smiled.

If you are reading this Pauline Lake, I am dead. I will leave it to you to decide whether or not to publicize what I did. By the way I should mention that whatever piece of jewellery you chose, it would be valuable enough to get rid of your little problem.

Mrs Lake didn't feel the same way as Emily though, but it was time to sell the house and blue heart and set up a little cake shop, perhaps by the sea. Curtain Crescent wasn't a place she wanted to be.

Unexpected Inheritance

The house was much bigger than I'd expected. In fact it was a mansion. That was the good news. The bad news was that it was in extreme disrepair. I didn't have enough money to buy a sandwich, let alone renovate such an impressive property. I'd left in a hurry and hadn't managed to get to a bank.

I walked beyond the boarded up windows, past the magnificent entrance and came to the back of the building. There attached to the back, was a tiny house. I searched through the bunch of keys and found one that opened the door. This must have been an employee's residence. It was basic but habitable. There was one large bedroom upstairs and a small living room, kitchenette and bathroom downstairs. My spirits lifted. This would do me just fine for the time being.

I slung my bag down on the old sofa and decided to explore the considerable grounds. They were beautiful and I could see several heavily laden apple trees a short walk away. 'Lunch sorted,' I thought and to be truthful it would be dinner and breakfast as well. The garden had a lawn leading to a small area of trees. As the garden sloped downwards I came across a tributary trickling over rocks.

I didn't deserve such a beautiful place to live, but as nobody knew about my unexpected inheritance, it was a safe place to stay for the time being. I knew I was being a coward running away, but when my boss found out that I'd paid the money for the new stock of cars into the wrong account, he would kill me. It was a genuine mistake. There had been no intention to profit by it at all. I'd called the bank as soon as I'd realized my mistake, but the clerk had laughed and told me I should've checked the details before pressing the button. £57,000 gone in an instant. Mr Green would have me prosecuted for fraud. I was in deep trouble.

My stomach rumbled. Obviously two apples were not enough to satisfy my hunger. I saw a patch of nettles in the corner of the grounds. Nettle soup; that might be a bit more filling, so I started to gather some, pulling my sleeves down to protect my hands.

I found some old stock cubes in the cupboard, a jar of coffee and some tinned beans. It felt like I was going to have a feast. The nettle soup was disgusting. I can honestly say I've never tasted anything like it before. Still, I mustn't grumble. The coffee was good.

In the evening I decided to explore the big house. The first few rooms were largely bare, with little furniture. Had my relative, Ethel Edenbridge, actually lived here? The rooms were magnificent with high ceilings and there were one or two large paintings on the wall, which I suspected might be worth a bob or two.

On the first floor I found a small set of rooms that were comfortably furnished. This was where Ethel must have spent her days. There were several pictures that looked to me like Picasso's. I looked more closely. I'm no expert but I'd studied art at college. If they weren't genuine they'd still fetch something. They were such good quality. I opened the next room and there were hundreds of paintings, stacked all around the room against the wall.

That night as I lay in my strange bed in the tiny house, I realized that this was a defining moment in my life. I could go back and face the music with Mr Green. If I sold all the paintings I might be able to pay him back a good proportion of the money I'd caused him to lose. Alternatively, I could use the sale money to do the big house up and live in what can only be described as splendour. I could even copy those pictures before I sold them and have a go at making replicas, for my own use, so the house would keep some of its history. It was a hard choice.

By morning I knew there was no choice. I would always regret running away and if Mr Green got most of his money back, perhaps he wouldn't prosecute. I rung his number but I didn't get the chance to speak.

'Ahh, there you are, Jackson. I said to my wife you'd be in touch. Don't worry lad. The bank's been on to me and I know you tried to put right your little mistake. They're happy to sort it out. All they need is your signature. I might get someone to check your transfers in future lad, but there's no hard feelings.'

'I don't understand. Why do they need my signature?' I asked.

'Because you transferred the money for the new cars into your bank account. Didn't you realize?'

'No, Sir. I thought I'd reversed two numbers or something and all that money had gone goodness knows where. I'll be along to sort it out later this morning.'

'That's fine lad.'

I took the train to a town forty miles north of where I was and went to the library and waited for a computer to become free. Then I transferred £57,000 to the garage's account. Mr Green could still prosecute me, but he'll have to find me first.

I decided to sell those pictures one at a time and start doing the place up. And I'd start painting again. I'd always wanted to be an artist and now I had the space to do it and I wouldn't have to work for the dubious Mr Green again. In the meantime I'd find a cash machine and draw enough money out to buy some groceries. Life was full of hope.

The Long Driveway

Harry Blaze made his way up the long driveway, noticing the borders needed attention and roses needed pruning. He'd learned his gardening skills in prison, but had decided that if he was going to turn his life around, he needed to go straight. Just before he left prison, he'd been offered an interview for a gardening post at this beautiful, if intimidating, grand house. He rang the doorbell.

An old style manservant with greyish skin, and wrinkles that would have done a prune proud, answered the door.

'You're expected, Sir. Please come in. I'm Barnaby. Have been with Lady Joyce for forty years.'

The old man smiled at Harry, a warm smile that changed his face completely. It eased Harry's nerves a little.

Harry was shown into a large sitting room with high ceilings and faded, worn furniture. Seated near an ornate coffee table was a grey haired lady, wearing tiny round spectacles.

'Mr Blaze, M'Lady,' said Barnaby.

'Would you bring us some coffee and biscuits, Barnaby? Thank you.'

Harry shuffled awkwardly. He'd never been in a house so grand and stately.

'Oh, do sit down my boy. Now, I understand you've been away and during your time have trained as a gardener. Your reference says that you have a natural talent. I used to be the same you know.'

Harry's eyes scanned the room, nervously. He so wanted this job; to make a new start and not return to prison, but his eyes rested on the photographs set out in rows and there was a picture of his mother. *What an earth was that about?*

Lady Joyce was speaking, 'I can see you're admiring the photo frames. Yes they're silver and you need to know I know exactly how many there are. Seventeen, and if any go missing you'll be out of here quicker than you know.'

Harry looked at her with resignation and then back to the picture, he was sure was his mother.

'I can only count sixteen and anyway, you contacted me to offer me a job. I thought you were giving me a real chance.' He stood up. 'I was obviously wrong. You just want someone as a whipping boy.'

'Oh do sit down, Harry. I know you want the job.'

He was about to sit down, when Barnaby tottered in with the coffee. Harry took the heavy tray and placed it on the table. Barnaby shuffled out of the room but Harry knew the footsteps stopped outside the door.

'Let me tell you about the job,' said Lady Joyce. 'You'll be completely in charge of the garden. It will be up to you to bring it back to its former glory. It needs a lot of work, but you'll be paid well and there's a flat over the garage you can have for free.'

'That all sounds good.'

'And you can come and eat with me in the evenings and keep me company.'

'That seems a bit odd, if you don't mind my saying so. Do you eat with Barnaby too?'

'Of course not, he's my employee.'

Harry grimaced, 'So will I be.'

'Oh dear,' said Lady Joyce, 'I was hoping to have a bit of time to get to know you before we came to this point. I suppose I'd better explain.' She paused.

'How do I put this nicely? I can't. I had a daughter – your mother. The thing is I have no heir to pass this place on to, except you. I'm sorry to say your mother had no morals. She hooked up with a most unsuitable man. A member of the lower class, no less.' she whispered. 'Well I couldn't have the family name brought into disrepute, so I asked her to leave. Harsh I know but they were different times back then. That's why you ended up in an orphanage. I couldn't bring her child back here. What would people have said?'

Harry thought about his childhood. Lots of noise and people around, but no-one of his own.

'She was never designed to be a good mother, you know and your father skedaddled,' said Lady Joyce.

'Did you know she came to see me in prison before she died? She knew she hadn't got long and it had taken her months to find me. She cried and apologised for letting me down, but told me I could still make a good life for myself and that's what I'll do. She told me all about how she fell in love with my father. They were childhood sweethearts,' said Harry.

'Well, it's all in the past now. I'm trying to make amends. I'm offering you a chance to get back on your feet and become part of the family.'

Harry felt both sadness and anger that this woman had ruined his mother's life and damaged his. All his life he'd wanted a family, but no-one came to adopt him. The local gang had become his family and soon he was in trouble with the law.

'I don't think so, Lady Joyce. I only met my mother for an hour, but I could tell she was warm hearted and kind. I don't think I want to be part of your family,' said Harry, knowing that his chance of getting another such perfect job offer was now next to zero.

With that he took his phone out, walked over to the pictures and snapped any photographs that had his mother in.

'There's still sixteen frames,' he said as he strode over and opened the door.

Barnaby stood back to let him out.

As Barnaby followed him to the front door he said, 'Your father is my son. 'He's a good man. Lives in the village.'

Harry turned and looked at the old man.

'Why did he desert my mother in her hour of need?' Harry asked.

'He was serving in the army, abroad. He didn't know about you until recently. Come and meet him. I'm sure you'll like him.'

Harry smiled. He might have some family after all. He gave Barnaby his arm and they walked slowly, away from the imposing house, along the extensive drive towards the village, together.

The Trouble with Weasels

When you're a mother, you spend years trying to protect your children from all outside dangers and hardships, but when your children grow up, you have to let them make their own mistakes. It's so hard not to give them your more experienced opinion, but I try my best to be quietly supportive.

My daughter, Cassie, is one of the kindest and warmest human beings you could meet. She always sees the best in people, which is a wonderful virtue, but I worry about how easily she could get hurt. Watching her start dating is something I'd have liked to ban, but she'd hate me and of course, I have no right.

At first, Edward Weasel seemed to be a charming young man. My daughter fell for him, as only the young can, with total commitment, which would have been admirable, if only it had been for another cause, like saving the planet. Who has a name like Weasel anyway? Edward said he was twenty eight and he certainly looked that age until you looked more closely. His reddish brown hair was just a little too even, as though it was dyed, and although he gave an appearance of height, I noticed that his shoes had a subtle heel to compensate for short legs. Now don't get me wrong, I have nothing against short, older men, but I am quite averse to men who pretend to be something they're not. If his appearance didn't come up to scratch, that was the least of my worries.

'Don't you think he's wonderful, Mum?' my daughter asked.

'As long as he makes you happy, I'm happy,' I lied, but I wasn't at all happy.

I couldn't put my finger on what it was I didn't like about him until about a month later. My brother was throwing a party for the rich and famous. He's a successful film director. He always invited us to his parties and we never go. When folk are wearing top notch clothes and jewellery that makes your eyes water, it makes you feel like you're a country bumpkin, when you turn up in your best Marks and Spencer frock. Okay, I admit it, I'm an inverted snob, but my brother really isn't. He's smart and direct and he always sees things very clearly. We received and politely declined the latest party invitation. A few days later Cassie cornered me.

'Mum, do you think we could un-decline that party invitation to Uncle Derek's? Edward would really like to go.'

My first instinct was to say no, but when Cassie has set her heart on something, I find it hard not to give in.

The night of the party arrived and I have to say Cassie looked exceptional. She'd found a beautiful, knee length, silk dress in a charity shop. It oozed style and class, but when Edward turned up, he was obviously disappointed in how she looked.

'I assumed you'd dress up a bit more; you know a long dress,' he muttered, thinking I couldn't hear.

'I think she looks absolutely gorgeous,' I said. 'Now don't be a jerk. Off you both go'.

I know I shouldn't have said anything, but how could he criticise her? Edward did have the grace to go red, but I'm not sure if he was ashamed of himself or angry that I'd called him out on his rudeness.

The next day I asked Carrie how the party had gone.

'It was fabulous, Mum. Uncle Derek introduced me to everyone as his favourite niece. He whispered, *we won't tell anyone that you're my only one*.' She laughed and without hesitating said, 'Can I bring William home for tea later?'

'William?' I queried. 'What happened to Edward?'

'Oh, I dumped him,' she said. 'When we left here, we had a row. Not the best start to the evening. He didn't like you calling him a jerk,' she smiled.

'I'm sorry. I shouldn't have said that, but you looked so beautiful and you'd taken such care.'

'Anyway, we agreed to put it behind us. He was so eager to go to the party and I wanted us to have a good time.'

'So, what happened then?' I asked.

'When we arrived, I introduced him to Uncle Derek, and he seemed to forget I was there. He stood in front of me and actually stood on my foot. I mean anyone could do that, but you check the person you hurt is all right, only he didn't. Then later, he was trying to impress Juliet Snow – you know from the Northlander's show, and he actually snapped his fingers at William to bring us some drinks. I was so embarrassed. Juliet was lovely. She thanked William for the drink and told him she'd started her working life as a waitress, so she knew how hard he had to work.'

'She does sound kind.'

'Then Edward said I should go and speak to my uncle, because he obviously wanted Juliet to himself, but she linked my arm and said that was a good idea. She had something she wanted to talk to Uncle Derek about, so we left Edward standing on his own.'

'So, is it really all over with Edward?' I asked.

Cassie put her arms round me, 'Of course it is. He wheedled himself into so many conversations; interrupting when people were talking. I was feeling bad about bringing him, but Juliet Snow told me, that's the problem with weasels. They're flibbertigibbets, who scurry around everywhere, but have no worthwhile purpose.'

Cassie laughed as she went upstairs to get ready for William. I sighed. Derek had been right as usual. When I'd rung him to ask what I should do about Cassie's interest in Edward, Derek had told me to let them come to the party. His thoughts were that if Edward was not a genuine person, he would almost certainly show himself up, amongst the rich and famous.

I wonder what William is like.

Martha's Dilemma

The small, stone church was off the beaten track, at the top of a gently sloping hill. It was damp, with broken roof tiles and a couple of the smaller windows were patched up with card and plastic. The new part-time vicar, Reverend Beecham, had lost his enthusiasm or maybe his faith, and showed little interest in either the church or the village it served.

Martha tried her best to brighten the place up. She'd cleaned and sprayed air freshener to mask the damp odour; then she placed the recently bought, bright yellow chrysanthemums into the flower holders. She felt there was no excuse, not to make St Joseph's a welcoming place, even if the congregation was often limited to five, frail octogenarians. Idly she wondered what would happen to the church when they were all gone.

Perhaps Martha had taken longer than usual cleaning the building, as twilight had turned to darkness and the churchyard only had one light at its entrance. She had no reason to rush home and liked to keep herself busy. It helped her cope with life's challenges. She stuffed the large key into her oversized handbag and retrieved her tiny torch. One thing that could be said about Martha was she was always prepared. The torch's beam made a misty yellow circle on the ground in front of her, as she made her way towards the entrance. Out of the corner of her eye she saw a black shape on the ground. She shone the dim light onto it and recognised, almost immediately, Reverend Beecham's body. He was face down on the grass but his head was turned sideways; the back of which was caved in, and a pool of blood seeped into the earth.

Martha found she was holding her breath as she stooped down to check his pulse, but she couldn't find any. She reached into her bag for her large digit phone, when she heard footsteps. It wasn't clear whether the footsteps were coming towards her or not, but she decided to run, which was not an easy task, even for a spritely eighty-one year old.

Soon the churchyard was filled with police, tape and lights.

Martha opened up the building and was sitting on the pew at the back. She was fingering a silver button in her pocket, rolling it round and round. It was smooth at the back and had an anchor on the front. It distracted her while she waited to be interviewed.

'How ironical that the place was now so busy, when it was nearly empty while Reverend Beecham was alive?' she thought and almost smiled.

P.C. Katy Campbell came and joined her and asked all sorts of questions.

'When was the last time you saw Reverend Beecham?' she said.

'It must've been around five, but he was keen to get off and I hadn't finished my work.'

'Was it normal for him to leave you in the church, alone?'

'Quite normal. I spent more time here than he did.'

'Are you employed by the church?'

'No, I'm a long serving volunteer. Must be nearly thirty years I've worked here.'

'And did you have your own key?'

'Yes, he and I both have one and I think there's a spare, somewhere,' replied Martha.

'Would you say he was a popular man? Did he have any enemies that you know of?'

'Well popular isn't quite the word I'd use. I think somewhere along the line he'd lost his mojo. Perhaps I might describe him as a bit depressed, not that he ever said anything to me,' said Martha. 'Most people didn't really like him, but I don't know of anyone who hated him.'

By the time she'd finished answering all the questions she felt exhausted and was pleased to be taken home.

Reverend Beecham hadn't been a kind man. He'd seemed bitter about being moved suddenly from his previous parish, although nobody at St Joseph's knew why he'd been transferred to them. He was absent from most of the village events where he'd be expected to attend, and services, when he remembered to turn up, were delivered in a dull, flat voice.

The only time he'd shown any enthusiasm for life was when Martha's son had died. Reverend Beecham was round to comfort Tracy Townsend every day, offering help and support. His attentiveness had surprised and irritated Martha. Surely he didn't think a grieving widow in her thirties would be interested in a sloppy, balding man in his fifties? Tracy was extremely vulnerable and suffering not only from grief, but shock. The situation went on for several weeks until one day, Tracy's son, Tony, came home from school and found his mother chucking the Reverend out of their house. Martha, who was looking out of her window, had never seen Tony so angry. He was usually a quiet, studious boy, who wouldn't say boo to a goose, but that afternoon, he'd actually chased the Reverend away from the house. In due course Tracy made a formal complaint to the Bishop about Reverend Beecham's inappropriate behaviour, but nothing had been heard about that since. Maybe the Bishop was looking for another 'out of the way' living to ship him off to.

Once on her own, Martha began to wonder if she should've said more to the police. She hadn't told any lies, but she hadn't told them everything she knew. She'd told them Reverend Beecham wasn't popular, not like the lovely Reverend Harris, who'd preceded him. She should've told them about Tracy's problems, but then maybe it wouldn't come out, and why should

Tracy be burdened with questions with all she was going through?

More concerning was the button. She'd picked it up from the scene of crime. She'd recognised it immediately because she'd bought the set of them at a second-hand stall at the church fete, last year. She'd bought them for two pounds because nobody had realized they were real silver. Martha had sewn them onto her grandson's latest coat and he'd been so pleased with them. She placed the button on the table and looked at it closely. Then she washed it in as solution of bleach, rinsed it, dried it and placed it in her button box, which contained hundreds of other buttons. Tomorrow she'd slip round to his house and sew it on again.

No-one could expect her to shop her own grandson. Tony was such a gentle young man. He'd just lost his dad and had witnessed that creep try it on with his mother at a time of extreme grief. Obviously, Martha thought murder was wrong, but Tony was only fifteen and had his whole life ahead of him.

Family Ties

Barry and Sally were walking along the pier, watching the tide going out. They were killing time before meeting up with family. Under the pier a lot of rubbish had collected. It didn't look too bad when covered with water, but now he could see all the gunge. Barry peered through the slatted floor and was saddened by the amount of rubbish, when he realized there were two human arms sticking up, out of the debris, one with the puppet, Punch on and one with the puppet, Judy.

Barry saw the gruesome sight and passed out, smashing down on the wet pier floor. When he awoke Sally was leaning over him, calling his name. He tried to sit up.

'Just stay lying down for a moment,' she said.

He thought, *what a wimp I look now.*

'Your brother told me all about your childhood. I do understand.'

'No, you don't. There's a body down there,' he said.

Sally peered through the wooden floor. She took out her phone and called the police. Meanwhile two waiters from the cafe came out and helped Barry inside. Soon he and Sally were brought a welcome pot of tea.

Outside the wind blew, the sea was rocky and the crowds were gathering, but the pier security personnel stood guard on the pebbles below, preventing people contaminating the scene. The police arrived and the crowds were dispersed, but Barry and his girlfriend stayed in the cafe drinking their tea.

'What did my brother tell you about our childhood?' he asked eventually.

'He told me that your parents were often absent at work, and left you in the hands of your older sister, Estelle, who didn't want to look after you, so she would scare you both rigid with her Punch and Judy puppets.

Punch literally beat you both and Judy made cruel and unkind comments. He told me how he pretended to be asleep and you took most of the beatings and how you both used to sob your hearts out silently when she left the room.'

Barry shook his head. He'd really hoped that Sally would see him as a strong man and now she would always know how feeble he was.

The door opened and a gust of cold air announced the arrival of the police. Inspector Denby sat down across the table from them.

'Well sir, I understand you were the first person to see the body. Is that right, Mr Stanford?'

'I just saw the arms and the puppet heads,' said Barry.

'Tell me why were you looking through the flooring?'

'I don't know. I just always do. I live round the corner. I suppose it's a remnant of when I came here as a child.'

'And then you passed out. It must have been an awful shock for you, to have made you pass out. I don't suppose you knew the victim.'

'I told you. I only saw the arms and the puppets and everything was covered in gunge and rubbish.'

'Well now Mr Stanford I have a picture of the woman to whom those arms belonged. She is deceased and not too clean. Are you up to taking a look?'

Barry took a deep breath and nodded. Inspector Denby held out his phone. Barry could feel the blood draining from his face. He grabbed the table to stop himself passing out again.

'Do you recognise the victim, Mr Stanford?'

'Yes Sir. I do. It's my sister, Estelle. I haven't seen her in ten years.'

Sally was looking shocked, but she reached out and touched his hand.

'Mr Stanford, I think we should continue our chat down at the police station. We don't know how she died or how many hours ago it was, yet, but I think we should take both your statements. Shall we go?'

'He's recovering from fainting,' said Sally. 'I think he should be going to hospital.'

'Oh, I'll get our doctor to take a look at him. Don't you worry, Miss.'

The journey to the police station didn't take long. Barry went straight in to see the doctor, while a Detective Constable took Sally's statement. Sally told her, what time they'd arrived at the pier and that they'd been going to meet other family members but, Estelle, Barry's sister hadn't been invited. She mentioned how Barry had been looking through the floor of the pier and passed out. When he'd told her there was a body, she'd immediately called the police.

Meanwhile the doctor had examined Barry's vital signs and said he could be interviewed, but he had banged his head as he fell and that they must keep an eye on him, in case of concussion. Barry's brother, Mike and sister-in-law arrived and were also questioned. Eventually they were allowed to go home for the night.

The next day the scene of crime report came back, which showed that Estelle had climbed up on the ironwork below the pier, possibly with the puppets on her hands. There was no evidence of her being hurt by anyone. It seemed likely that the spray and the wind had caused her to lose her footing. The police couldn't imagine why she'd been climbing, after all she wasn't a teenager.

Sally said, 'She probably was going to frighten the boys for a bit of fun.'

'Well she certainly did that,' said Inspector Denby. 'I'm sorry for your loss. We'll be in touch about the release of the body.'

Much later that night Barry was walking along the beach with Mike. They paused as they passed under the pier, which had been completely cleared of debris.

'It's over now,' said Mike.

'But what was she doing here and why was she climbing up the pier's structure? I don't understand.'

'She was out to blight our day. Probably found out we were meeting up, through Mum, and was annoyed we'd not invited her. She was out to give you a shock. She knew more than anybody how scared you are of Punch and Judy.'

'But why did she fall?'

'Because the iron work was slippery and she was wearing puppets on her hands. I want you to know, I didn't do anything. I just shouted at her to get down. She turned to see who was yelling and fell. I couldn't help her. She fell into the muddy water onto a pile of rubbish and she disappeared except for her arms, which stuck up at right angles. Probably trying to keep the puppets dry.'

'But surely she could've been saved?' said Barry.

'I really don't think so. It was a massive fall, and anyway she taught us how to keep silent, whatever pain she put us through. We can get on with our lives now. She won't hurt us again.'

Barry looked at his brother with understanding. He wouldn't tell the police what his brother had said. Now he'd met Sally, it was time to move away, and start a new family with a happier narrative.

The Ring of Mystery

Bev hadn't been out for months, but the days were warmer now and although she had no idea how to go on, she did feel up to walking around her garden. At the back of the garden they owned a field. She corrected herself; she owned a field. Peter, her boyfriend had walked out and left her. Her whole life had been turned upside down. The house was already in her name. She'd paid for everything as he tried to build up his business.

When he'd walked out on her to marry Fiona, he'd graciously said,' I don't want anything from here. I'm going to be so bloody rich you're not going to believe it.'

Bev hadn't appreciated it at the time, but now she realized how lucky she'd been not to have to sell-up and move somewhere smaller.

With her old and trusty flask of tea she wandered to the end of the garden and into the field. It was unsurprisingly a mess. The Blackthorn bushes in the middle of the field had flourished and were taking over the top part of the field. The grass was high, too high, but there was a pathway near the edge. Bev decided she would take the chair from the tiny hide she'd built last year and go and drink her tea and watch the birds. She'd seen a buzzard flying the other day and there were crows and magpies, as well as robins, dunnocks and thrushes.

She turned a corner and came across an amazing sight. It was a circle made from thin Blackthorn branches. How on earth had that got there? This was private land. She went up to it and examined it. It was beautiful and perfect. Almost unreal. She hesitated to step through it. What if it was a time portal and took her centuries back into the past or perhaps even more frightening, to the future? What rubbish, she told herself firmly and in any case, what was there for her here? She slipped her small frame nimbly through the circle.

On the other side the grass was cut and she could hear the sound of a small child chattering.

'No, here's one for you, Mr. Ted, and one for you, Janet.'

The child looked up and ran over to Bev, excitedly.

'I was hoping you'd come one day. The Queen of the castle,' she said and curtseyed. 'Your throne is this way.'

Bev couldn't help but smile. The throne was a tiny plastic stool and she wondered if she sat on it, if she'd be able to get up.

'The Queen would like to know, who you are, what you're doing here and where's your mummy?'

The little girl's face fell and Bev thought that tears might follow.

'I'm not cross with you,' she added quickly.

'I'm Lilly. I live next door. Mummy's working. She likes me to play outside when she's working.'

'Does she realize you're playing on my land and not in your garden?'

'Maybe not, but Daddy knows. He knocked on your door on Saturday. He cut the grass in the top part of your field when he came for his visit.'

'Why did he do that?'

'Mummy said he couldn't stay in the house with us and he hadn't any money to take me anywhere, so he got out his gardening things. He thought you wouldn't mind if he helped you with the field. He said he'd do the other half next weekend.'

Bev sat down on the throne and listened to Lilly chattering away. She was an enchanting child. Eventually Lilly offered to share her sandwich.

'Don't you go home for lunch?'

'Mum's very busy. I'm okay as long as I'm with Mr. Ted and my favourite doll, Janet. It's been a lovely day with you being here.'

'Shall I phone your mum and ask if you can come round to my house for lunch?'

'Oh yes please,' Lilly said, holding out her arm, which bore a plastic bracelet with a telephone number.

After the call they picked up Mr. Ted and Janet and made their way back to the house. As they came to the mystery ring of blackthorn twigs, Bev admired its beauty.

'Dad made that. He said when you go back through the ring you go back to normal life. This side is our play place.'

'Well, he's very clever.'

'He had to wear gloves when he made it, because of the prickles and we have to be careful as we go through.'

They both safely climbed through the ring. As they did, Bev realized the truth of the ring. She was going back to reality but something had happened on the other side. She felt stronger. A small child had enjoyed her company. She was still a worthwhile person. Life could go on.

Ambition

I wouldn't say that my job was exactly boring, because dealing with the public makes every day different. I work in an employment agency and help people to find work. Don't ask me how I came to be working there because I can't remember. There were three of us who started there together. Annie left over two years ago when she gave birth to little Becky. Suzanne took the other route. She now manages the branch. Here am I, a good worker, turning up every day, but still doing the same thing after five years.

I meet lots of interesting characters and sometimes it changes people's lives, finding them a good job. You can match people's talents to the skills required for some jobs and that can be very satisfying.

Angel Martin comes in every few weeks. She usually is employed in an office and is always enthusiastic at the idea of starting a new job. Unfortunately, Angel hasn't quite worked how to deal with working with others. She rubs folk up the wrong way and then either is fired or walks out, usually not quietly. Still, it keeps me busy. Luckily there is plenty of work around, so she earns a living even if it isn't exactly continuous.

'Just for a change, I've got a job for you.' Angel told me one Monday, having recently retreated from yet another place of work.

'Oh yes and what might that be?' I asked.

'My sister is getting married next month and they would like you to play the piano at their reception,' Angel replied.

I smiled. This was not an unusual request, although normally I played for friends and family. I had no idea that Angel knew I loved playing the piano. Perhaps she'd heard me play at my regular two-hour slot at one of the local restaurants on a Saturday. The pay was minuscule but it was worth it for the lovely free meals and I really enjoyed it.

'Do say yes,' Angel pleaded as she handed me over a list of beautiful love ballads that the happy couple wanted.

'It will be a pleasure,' I said.

I'd never been known to turn down a chance to play. We then spent the next half hour discussing why she'd been slung unceremoniously out of her last place of work.

The following Saturday, Suzanne came to have lunch at The Blue Parrot restaurant, while I was doing my turn. There was a low buzz of people chattering but I focused on the music, as did quite a few customers. Suzanne was looking stunning as usual in her designer jeans and white heeled shoes. She had with her a very handsome young man by the name of Dennis. It was obvious that they were in love as they couldn't take their eyes off each other and held hands between courses. I practised some of the love ballads that I was going to play at the wedding of Angel's sister and they seemed a popular choice. Once or twice, I glanced over to Suzanne and Dennis and wondered why it was that Annie had her baby and Suzanne had her Dennis and I wasn't doing very well at anything. I began to feel quite melancholy until the manager came over and whispered in my ear,

'Something lively next. You're sending the customers to sleep.' I could have been cross, but he said it with a smile.

The next Monday I booked an appointment with Suzanne to discuss how I could get promoted in my job. She took it all very seriously and told me about all the courses she'd passed and the hours of overtime that she'd put in and asked if that was what I was prepared to do? I said yes immediately and then wondered how much it would interfere with my music. Suzanne went away to find me some brochures about courses, in human resources.

At lunchtime I went to have a sandwich with Annie and Becky. They looked so happy. Annie couldn't afford designer jeans, but she looked great in a beautiful hand embroidered jumper and long gathered skirt. Becky wore a standard romper suit, with a tiny jacket and frilly pink hat.
'So is motherhood all it's made out to be?' I asked.
'Oh yes and more so. I can't imagine a world without Becky now. It's fascinating to see her grow. Every day she learns something different and the changes come so quickly. I'm so happy,' enthused Annie. I started to think about getting married and having a baby. Now that would be nice.

That night as I slept fitfully, I dreamed I was playing the piano with a baby in a sling round my neck and my arms had grown incredibly long, so that I could reach the keys. In the next instant, I was surrounded by papers, studying, and the piano was covered in layers of dust. I woke up more confused than ever.

The next morning, I decided that I must take a grip of myself. I wasn't sure about going for promotion and I didn't even have a boyfriend, so having a baby was going to be a bit difficult. I decided that I'd just get on with the things I had to do. In my lunchtime I rushed to the Chilton Hotel, where the wedding reception was going to be and asked if I could come and have a practice. Every piano has a different sound and I wanted to be comfortable with it on the big day. We booked a couple of hours for after work that night.

During the afternoon, I had a call from the manager of The Blue Parrot who asked if I would play for a theme evening on a Thursday evening every week. I said yes with my usual enthusiasm. Then I set about finding a job where Angel's temper could be tolerated. Perhaps she needed to be outdoors and doing something more physical, which would use up her energy. It just so happened that there were some seasonal vacancies for helpers at the local zoo, so I thought I'd see if she'd give it a go. After all, if she didn't like it, she could leave!

That evening I took my music to the Chilton and settled down for a good play. The room was large, with high ceilings and thick plush carpet. There was virtually no one around, which was fine. I stroked the beautiful mahogany grand piano in the same way that some people would stroke their beloved cats and then settled down to play. Time passed as the music flowed through my fingers and I played on. When I finally stopped all the people in the restaurant gave me a round of applause and the hotel manager handed me thirty pounds and asked if I would do a regular evening of music for them. I hadn't even noticed the restaurant fill up.

I met Ben the following Saturday at the Blue Parrot. He was with Suzanne and Dennis.
'You should let Ben come and play alongside you. He plays a mean double bass.' Suzanne said. Ben smiled awkwardly.
What did Suzanne think she was playing at? This was my job. You couldn't just bring your friends to join in. It was then that I started to think about what was really important to me. Ben didn't stop for lunch and Suzanne looked at me crossly. I played my music and went into my own little world.

I noticed Ben later in the week at the Chilton Hotel and went up to speak to him.

'I thought I'd come and hear you play, when you weren't having me foisted on you by our dear Suzanne. I can tell you really love your music,' he said, 'Why on earth are you working in an employment agency?'

'I still have to pay the rent.' I replied.

'You could teach music in schools or give private lessons, as well as your regular sessions at The Blue Parrot and here. You could advertise to play at weddings and parties. You could play with me?' The question hung in the air for a few moments. I relented, after all he was incredibly good looking and he obviously shared my love of music.

'Would you like to come to my flat on Sunday morning, with your double bass?' I asked and he gave a smile that lit up his face.

The bells of the church were chiming in the distance and I'd been playing for about half an hour, when he arrived and set up his instrument. We did play well together. He knew a lot of the music I knew and we immersed ourselves in the flowing notes that transport you away to other places. We only stopped when somebody's tummy rumbled very loudly!

In the weeks that followed life was busy. I played at Angel's sister's wedding and that was beautiful. The bride was exquisite and everyone was dressed in their finery. Playing at the Blue Parrot and the Chilton on such a regular basis made me increase my repertoire and Ben challenged me to work at more complex music.

I hadn't had time to decide about going for promotion and it was far too early days with Ben to be thinking about marriage and a baby, but I still had a big decision to make. Did I have the courage to give up my day job and follow my heart? What if I couldn't earn enough by playing music to pay the rent?

The next Tuesday the office was closed because some new cables had to be fitted. There was no chance of seeing Ben because he was teaching music to children at a local secondary school. I hadn't seen Angel for a while and was missing our little chats so I took myself off to the local zoo. When I found her, she was sitting with a snake around her neck, explaining to a group of young children how the snake sheds it's skin and that not all snakes are dangerous. I stood back and watched. Angel was totally engrossed in her work.

Later we had coffee in the zoo's utilitarian cafe. She loved her work because she was working with animals and every day was different. At last she didn't feel so claustrophobic. Then we talked about my work.

'You should go for it,' Angel pronounced. 'If it doesn't work out there will always be other jobs and if you don't do it, you'll always wonder if you could.'

I left her with my mind buzzing. In my heart I knew that I didn't want to be a career woman in the traditional sense and although I wanted a family eventually and possibly with Ben, I didn't want to be tied down just yet. There were new tunes to play and manuscripts to learn and audiences to tantalize.

That night I had a letter to write and next month I would start my new musical career.

Incomplete

My mother had passed away a month ago and I was sitting, surrounded by her possessions, sorting them into piles to go to the charity shop or to go to the tip. I didn't have space to keep much.

I picked up a white leather bible just like the one I owned. The inscription in the book was identical to my copy, except the name was different. Who was this Anna, and why was the book hidden in my mum's tin of memories that I'd found at the back of the wardrobe? I was certain that it had been written in my mum's writing but I had no-one I could ask. I decided I would keep the book. Idly I leafed through the pages and a yellowed photo fell to the ground. It was creased and grainy, slightly out of focus, in the way old photos can be, but there was my mother in her prime, sitting very upright on a sofa, with two babies. I knew one was me as I had a baby photo, but the other baby was identical.

What had my mum been through? And why had she never told me that I was a twin? Strangely it didn't really surprise me. I'd often felt incomplete, as though something was missing.

I wished I'd had a member of my family left to ask all these questions, but there was no-one. All gone now. I may be an adult, but I was also an orphan. The loneliness and grief threatened to overcome me, when the doorbell rang and broke into my thoughts.

My mum's neighbour was standing at the door.

'I thought you were still at it, so I've made tea and cake. C'mon over to mine. A break will do you good.'

I was going to politely decline, but she'd started walking back to her house. I grabbed my keys and bag and followed.

Hilary was a kind soul and I suspect missed Mum as much as I did. The tea and cake were welcome as I'd forgotten to eat lunch.

'Your mum left this letter for you. She told me what was in it, so if you need to chat, I'm here.'

I opened it carefully.

My dear Ella,

If you're reading this, I've gone, but there's still something I need to tell you.

When I was nineteen, I had you and Anna, your twin. We had no money. I don't mean we had little money; I mean we struggled to find enough money for food. We'd not expected twins and your dad and I decided that we couldn't afford to keep you both.

It was all agreed and arranged before the birth. I only had her for a week and then she was taken by the adoption agency. We struggled to feed and look after you, so I know we did the only thing we could at the time, but it was a decision that we both regretted.

I found Anna, when she was twenty and contacted her. Of course, your dad was long gone by then. I'm afraid she was bitter, said she hated me and wanted nothing to do with me. I don't blame her.

You've grown up to be a beautiful, intelligent young woman and we gave you everything we could. She lived with parents who never quite connected with her and they had their own baby soon after.

I've left the house to you alone, but if you make contact with her and she would speak to you, I would want you to share the proceeds with her. It's up to you. I've written her name and address on the back.

Whatever you decide is the right decision.
My love always
Mum xx

'Are you all right dear?' asked Hilary.
'Yes, I'm fine. It's a bit of a shock.'

'What are you going to do?'

'I shall go and find her, of course. She's my twin and my only living family.'

'I hope it turns out well, for you both, but remember you'll be okay if she doesn't want to know you. You've survived all these years without her.'

I found Anna working in an office and reluctantly she agreed to see me. It was strange to see someone sitting opposite me who looked like me.

'So, you're the favoured one. Lucky you,' she said.

'I expect you were just the one nearer the door,' I replied. 'Listen I know you've had a rough deal, but our parents are gone and I'd like us to be friends. What've you got to lose?'

We spent the next couple of months sorting out Mum's house and getting to know each other. She had the same sense of humour and taste in music as me. I gave her the bible I'd found with her name on and showed her Mum's letter.

I shared the proceeds of the house sale with her, happy to have found my twin, but the next day she was gone. She posted me back the Bible, ripped to shreds with a message.

One thing my childhood taught me is, I don't need family.

I don't blame her at all. I was the lucky one.

September Time

It was Saturday and I felt like lounging in bed and doing nothing. I looked in the mirror and saw a woman past her prime, with the hint of jowls and lines around her eyes. I knew if I dressed up and put on make-up, I could still make myself presentable, but my youthful beauty, was gone. When your husband leaves you, for not just a younger woman, but one twenty five years younger, you know you can't compete.

The house felt large, empty and unloved, but the children were both visiting tomorrow, so I needed to get on. I dusted and vacuumed and then dived into the shower. I don't know why but I put on some make-up, a pretty top and flattering trousers. Now all I had to do was some cooking to be ready for tomorrow.

I was halfway through making a giant lasagne when the doorbell rang. It was Gerald with his new wife, Sylvia.

'I was hoping we could come in and have a chat,' said Gerald meekly.

'We need to sort out the unfair settlement that was made at the time of the divorce,' said Sylvia in a harsh voice.

'It's not convenient,' I said, 'and the settlement we made was fair, and is between me and Gerald and nothing to do with you.'

'Well that's not quite true, is it?' said Sylvia. 'Gerald and I are living in poverty, while you have a four bedroomed house. It's hardly right.'

'Gerald?' I queried, wondering what he'd told her.

'We just want a friendly chat,' he said appealing to my better nature.

'You know who my solicitors are. Contact me through them,' I replied.

'I demand to come in and sort this out once and for all,' said Sylvia. 'Gerald owns half this house.'

'I own this house and if you push your way in, I'll call the police,'

'You wouldn't dare,' said Sylvia.

'Try me,' I said.

'Well you haven't heard the last of this,' she said as she backed off. 'We need the house. We're expecting twins and you're one person. You don't need a house this size.'

In fairness Gerald did look shame-faced.

'*Our* children are visiting tomorrow, Gerald,' I said. 'Why don't you pop in for a drink, around seven,' and then closed the door.

I surprised myself at standing up to Sylvia and I'd certainly surprised Gerald, but then my life was different now. I'd spent our marriage supporting him and doing my best for the family. Nothing had ever been about me. Gerald knew my solicitors, because I'd had a part-time job with them. Although a fully qualified solicitor, I'd worked as a legal clerk, as that had been the only part-time vacancy.

The next day, Martin arrived with Jasmine and their new baby, Lily. The house was looking smart and I'd prepared most of the food in advance.

'I've put you in the front bedroom, so you've got an en-suite and the little bedroom next door if Lily needs a quiet space.'

He kissed me on the cheek, while carrying up the travel cot. Jasmine was holding Lily.

'Come through Jasmine. I'll put the kettle on.' Soon, the empty house, was full and I felt happy again.

'Do you mind if I feed her in the living room, or would you rather I go upstairs?' asked Jasmine.

'You make yourself right at home. I'm so pleased to see you all and Linda's coming to stay over too. She's bringing her latest.'

While Jasmine drank her tea, I held my granddaughter for the first time. I can't tell you how thrilled I was. She was so tiny and soft. Martin made me laugh with tales of their journey and then Jasmine fell asleep. She was exhausted, after a long journey with a new baby.

'While she's asleep I wanted to ask you, if we could stay for a while. The house we were buying fell through and I don't want to rush and buy somewhere that we don't really like. We can move to one of the other bedrooms if you like.'

'Don't be silly. I put myself in the extension and I'm really comfortable there. It's where I usually sleep now. Nice and modern and no memories. Of course you can stay.'

Soon Linda turned up with Matthew. He was a good looking young man, with sandy hair and an intelligent look about him, dressed rather formally in a smart suit.

'I've made up your old bedroom, Linda. I hope that's okay for you both. There's a family bathroom opposite,' I explained to Matthew.

I spent the afternoon cuddling Lily and then went to get dinner ready. While I was putting on the last finishing touches, Linda came to find me.

'Do you like Matthew, Mum? I didn't want you to meet him until I was sure he's the one.'

'Well I've only just met him, but he seems lovely.'

'I thought you might think him too old for me.'

'If you're sure he's right for you, then I'm happy. Now could you take these through and tell everyone dinner is ready,' I said as I handed her the warm plates in a tea towel.

We were just finishing the fruit crumble and custard when Gerald arrived with Sylvia. I wasn't expecting Sylvia, but I wasn't going to show it. She was dressed in an elegant green chiffon dress that made me feel frumpy.

'Come on through and I'll get you both a drink,' I said.

There was a short silence from everyone and then Martin said, 'Hello Dad. Hello Sylvia. You know Jasmine, but this is Matthew, Linda's partner.'

Gerald looked him up and down and said, 'How old are you? Linda's only twenty two. You look almost old enough to be her father.'

Before anyone else could reply, Matthew raised an eyebrow and said, 'I'm twelve years older than she is, which is less than half the difference between you and Sylvia, I believe.'

'Fair point,' said Martin. Gerald winced.

'I don't need your approval, anyway,' said Linda.

Let's all sit in the lounge and I'll bring round some coffee,' I said, trying to smooth the awkward situation.

It didn't take long for Sylvia to move the conversation round to the unfairness of her situation.

'I know you all don't like me, because you think I took your father away from your mother, but we're living in a hovel compared to where your mother is living and we're expecting twins.'

'Well congratulations,' said Linda. 'We don't hate you, Sylvia. Dad made a decision to leave Mum. I'm sure if it hadn't been you, it would've been someone else. I thought you were living in that lovely bungalow behind the park.'

'We've been trying to talk to your mum about the unfair settlement. They're hardly comparable houses. She took advantage of your Dad, because he felt sorry for her.'

'Please don't talk about me as if I'm not here, Sylvia,' I said. 'Gerald and I split everything down the middle. He left me with a three hundred thousand pound mortgage which I didn't know how I'd pay, on a three hundred and fifty thousand pound house and I paid him half of the equity, which at that time I couldn't afford. We split all bank accounts and savings, even though both the children were still living with me and he paid no maintenance. We both agreed it was a fair settlement at the date of the official separation and we were both represented by lawyers.'

'Well how come you're so well off now?' said Sylvia. 'You obviously hid some savings.'

'When my wifely duties ended,' I replied calmly, 'I had no need to work part-time. The children went off to university and I was able to apply for a full-time position in a promoted post. I can prove that it all took place after my marriage ended, if I have to.'

'Of course you don't have to,' said Gerald. 'We made a fair agreement and of course it's a final agreement.'

Sylvia glared at Gerald.

'Well it all sounds fishy to me,' said Sylvia.

'I'm just going upstairs to feed Lily,' said Jasmine, who obviously felt embarrassed.

'And I thought I'd take a look at the garden, if that's all right,' said Matthew, getting up from the sofa.

'I think it's time we left. Gerald,' Sylvia called, as she too got up.

Gerald handed her the car keys. 'You take the car dear. I'll get a taxi. I'm just going to spend an hour with the children.'

Sylvia snatched the keys and marched out, slamming the front door behind her.

Everyone seemed to relax, even Gerald. I went round with the coffee pot and then we settled down.

Later when everyone was chatting, I slipped out to the kitchen and started loading the dishwasher and clearing away. Gerald appeared at the door.

'I'm sorry that Sylvia's accusing you of all sorts. I think she's really jealous, but I'm sure she'll be fine when the twins are born.'

'I want to be clear, that I'll always be civil to you, Gerald. Even though our family is grown I don't want them to see us at each other's throats, but I don't want to help you financially. This should be our September time. We should be going travelling, meeting up with friends, looking after the grandchildren together and none of that will ever happen because you snatched that from me. Strangely I don't blame Sylvia, but if she's ever going to come to family events in my home again, she needs to stop griping about how unfair her life is. Do you understand?'

'I did try to make her understand, honestly.'

'I'm sure you did, but you'll have to try harder. These twins will be related to Martin and Linda and Lily. We are all going to have to try to build a different relationship.'

When I'd finished clearing away, I poured myself a glass of wine and offered Gerald one. We sat on stools by the breakfast counter as we'd done so many times before. It seemed so natural.

'I am sorry I hurt you,' he said.

'You did, but it's in the past and I'm enjoying life now. Are you happy with the idea of twins when you're nearly seventy?'

'It wouldn't have been my choice. I was happy with our family, but I'll do my best for the twins, when they come. You're right. This should be our September time, but I've gone back to April, with an old body. Sylvia's not happy. She didn't want children. I thought she was on the pill, but life often throws a spanner in the works.'

It was a statement not a query.

'It does,' I said, 'but here's to the future, whatever it may hold.' We clinked our glasses and downed the last of the wine.

'By the way, how did you pay off the mortgage?' Gerald asked.

'Martin and Linda gave me all their savings and Martin gave me a considerable chunk of money from his wages every month, until my wages went up. Before you look horrified, I put them on the house and am paying them back. I'm a partner in the firm now. Who knew I had such earning potential?'

'That was a good solution.'

'It was. This house was their home and they wanted to stay here and now Martin, Jasmine and Lily are coming to live here for a while, which means the place will be a family home again.'

Everyone went off to bed and Gerald left. I switched off the lights and locked the doors. I was just climbing the stairs when the telephone rang. It was Gerald.

'Sylvia's left me. She put a note on the kitchen table. Said I was a loser and couldn't support her in the style she wished to become accustomed. There are no twins. It was just a ruse to get you to give up the house. What am I going to do?'

'Gerald, you're going to make yourself a cup of tea and thank the heavens that you won't be doing midnight feeds at your age. Tomorrow is the start of a new era. You'll learn not only can you cope on your own, you may find some benefits. And as long as you never entertain the idea that I'd welcome you back, you can come and spend some time with the children. Now goodnight.'

I took my tea up to the bedroom and sat at the dressing table to remove my makeup. I looked into the mirror again. I was still past my prime, but I didn't envy Sylvia or Gerald. Sylvia was obviously looking for a man she could sponge off. Goodness only knows why she picked Gerald. He had a good job, but was hardly rich. And Gerald was vain enough to think that beautiful young women were after him for his inherent charm or wisdom or some such rubbish.

No, I realized I was actually happy. I had family around me, an exacting but rewarding career and I was available for babysitting the next generation. I couldn't ask for more.

Lady in the Woods

Adrian shouted, 'Where are you boy? C'mon Rusty. Time to go,' but the Springer Spaniel ignored him.

He walked towards the scrabbling sound and saw Rusty in full digging mode. Earth was flying into the air with abandon, so he strode over to the dog, leaned down and hooked on the lead. As he went to pull Rusty out of the hole, the dog turned his face towards Adrian, with a bone in his mouth. There was no odour of decay or whiff of death, just the pleasant smell of freshly turned earth. He took a deep breath, pulled one of his gloves out of his pocket and put it on.

'Sit,' he commanded.

Rusty sat.

'Leave.'

Rusty lowered the bone to the ground, but his black eyes watched Adrian the whole time. He made a low growl as Adrian picked up the bone, tossed it at the dug over earth and said, 'Walk.'

As he made his way down from the mound, he headed towards town to report his dog's find of a human bone. Rusty bounded alongside him, without a care in the world.

Inspector Winsford cursed as the telephone cut into his dream. He'd been back at his old house, having dinner with his wife and children. He grabbed the phone.

'We've had an anonymous call from a phone box, Sir. The caller said that there's a body in Viking Woods. It's near the top of the mound, but off the path to the right. He said his dog dug up a bone - looked human.'

'It's probably an animal but we'll have to take a look. Find out which phone box and get any CCTV footage. Why didn't the caller want to give us his name? I'll meet you in half an hour at the scene.'

He slammed down the phone.

Curses, he thought. Why did he get a body on a Friday? He wasn't working this weekend whatever happened. He was going to his ex's barbeque to have some time with his kids. Nothing was going to stop him. He'd lost his wife, but he certainly wasn't going to lose his family.

Abandoning his car in the woodland car park he handed his keys to Constable Staples to re-park it.

'Morning Sir.'

'I'm glad you think so,' said Winsford, but smiled. He liked the constable. *Always straight forward and reliable,* he thought.

He went to pick up his protective suit and gloves from the van. Doctor Morgan joined him as the group started walking up the hill. She was a tall woman with an athletic build. He was pleased she chose to walk beside him and glad that he'd finally given up alcohol. He was losing the plumpness from his waist and he was fitter than he'd been in the last seven years.

'Why is it always dog walkers and joggers that find the bodies?' Inspector Winsford asked by way of making conversation.

She smiled. 'Someone get out of bed the wrong side this morning?'

'Not really, but don't you get tired of dealing with all this death and misery. There'll be some dark tale behind all this, that we'll either get to the bottom of, or not.'

'The way I look at it, is that the person who died has a story they want us to know about and we're helping them finish their story. If it weren't for the likes of you and me the dead would lose their voice.'

Very commendable, he thought. His positive outlook had gone walkabout since his wife left. Fundamentally he agreed with Helen Morgan, but just lately he'd been struggling with seeing the point to anything. As they arrived at the taped off area they stopped and put on the plastic overshoes. He could see his eager sergeant there ahead of him.

'I found the bone the dog dug up and secured the area. Otherwise I've not touched anything Sir. I thought I'd best wait for the forensic team,' said Sergeant Willis.

'Well done, Chris. We'll let them get on with it and we'll take a walk round the mound and take some photos.'

It took over two hours to recover the body from the ground. A lot of surrounding earth went with it.

'Anything you can tell me, Dr Morgan?' he asked as they were leaving.

'Not much Inspector. Female, around five foot four. There's some remnants of material and this necklace.' She held up a silver necklace in an evidence bag, which had a leaf shaped pendant.'

'No identification?'

'No, but the good news is she has teeth, so we should be able to trace her identity through local dentists, if of course she's local, otherwise it may take longer. Also, we should be able to extract DNA. You're going to have to be patient with this one.'

He nodded and turned away to answer his mobile.

'Nick, I'm just checking you'll be there tomorrow. I don't want the kids disappointed at the last moment.'

'Hi Jess, I'll be there. Promised, didn't I?'

'And you're going to be polite to Gerald or you're not welcome.'

'Of course I'll be polite. Whatever I think of him, Charlotte and Will love him. I'm not stupid you know. I blew my marriage because I worked all hours.' He took a deep breath. 'I'm really looking forward to it Jess.'

'Okay then but let's not play games. You blew your marriage because of the drink. Anyway that's in the past. See you tomorrow.'

Inspector Winsford looked round for Chris Willis and they started to walk back towards the car park.

'Let's get some food and then set up the information board.'

When he returned from the canteen the photograph of the body was up and the photos of the nearby area. Chris also had images of the material and the necklace.

'We know she was murdered because she was buried, so it can't have been a heart attack while out walking. I thought I'd get a couple of officers out visiting the jewellers in case anyone recognizes the necklace.'

'Good idea Chris and include the catalogues and online stores that sell jewellery. It was silver but it didn't look too expensive to me.' He moved along the board.

'Who's this guy?' said Inspector Winsford, pointing to a young man who hadn't been 'labelled' yet.'

'Just getting to him Sir. Constable Burton traced the phone box and CCTV images and this guy's our best bet for the anonymous informer. Nobody can identify him so far, so I thought I'd get this image out to everyone. Probably has nothing to do with the murder but there must be a reason he wouldn't give his name.'

'Excellent work Sergeant. I hope you've had some lunch.'

He walked towards his office.

'I'm going to search for a map of the area and look at ways that the murderer could get the body up the hill. Who's working on the missing person list?'

'We were just waiting for the Doc. to tell us how far to go back,' said Chris.

Inspector Winsford turned before his door. 'Let's go back ten years and get on with it now. We can change the search later when we get more information.'

'I just thought as the body's been in the ground a while it would be more economic to make a more precise search.'

'I understand your view Sergeant, but there are parents or children waiting somewhere for news.' He went into his room and closed the door.

'She's been dead for years. A few more days won't make any difference,' Chris muttered under his breath, but he went to arrange the missing person's search.

It was at ten to six when Inspector Winsford received a call from Doctor Morgan. 'We've identified our lady in the woods. She's Anne Curry of 17, Park Road. Last seen by the dentist on 3 May 2011 and so she can't have been dead more than four years. Bit of luck - he was the second dentist we called. Have a good weekend. Anne Curry will wait for justice.'

Nick Winsford picked up his briefcase and coat and went into the incident room.

'Stick this information on the board and we'll visit this address on Monday, first thing.' He went to leave but Sergeant Willis called to him.

'Shouldn't we go now or at least tomorrow? Aren't there parents or children waiting for news?'

'Good point, Sergeant,' said Winsford with a wry grin. 'But before we go blundering in, I want to know who lives at that address now, whether she was reported missing and any other background information on those at this address. I'm not working this weekend. I'm over in Bankiton visiting my children, so if you've any spare time...' he held his hand up in a wave as he left the room.

Chris shook his head and started to pack up his things.

The next day was sunny and bright. There was little breeze to ruffle the warming heat of the day.

'Your dad's here,' Jess called to the children, who were at the other end of the garden. 'And wonder of wonders you're on time and presentable,' she said to him.

'I promised,' he said handing her a bottle of good wine, which he hoped was an acceptable gift.

She took it without looking and plonked it down on a nearby table. Will ran up and gave Nick a big hug and Charlotte strolled towards him smiling and planted a kiss on his cheek. *When had she grown up?* he thought.

'Hi Nick,' she said.

'I'm not Nick to you, young lady. I'm Dad.'

'Gerald says we should call him Dad as he's doing the father role and you're more like a distant uncle.'

Nick Winsford could feel anger rising up through his body. He'd kill the little squirt.

'Charlie, he said no such thing. You shouldn't wind people up.' Jess turned to Nick and smiled at him, 'He will never take your place as their dad, nor does he want to.'

He breathed slowly and smiled back, 'Of course he wouldn't,' relieved that he hadn't actually done anything to regret.

'Charlie's always doing that. Thinks it funny,' said Will.

'No, I don't,' snapped Charlie.

Nick didn't want the day to start with a squabble, so he said, 'Right you two, lead me to the food. I haven't eaten in three weeks.'

They laughed and grabbed his hands.

He loved being with his children, and if being nice to Gerald was the price he had to pay, then he'd pay it. Charlie was almost as tall as her mum these days and had the same stunning looks. Will was small and wiry, unlike his dad, but there was still time for a growth spurt. Gerald was doing the cooking. He shook Nick's hand warmly.

'Good to see you, Nick. Now help yourself to the salads and then you can choose what you want to go with it.'

'Great Gerald. It all looks lovely.' Nick did his best to smile. This sleight, ineffectual, pretty man was all that stood between him and getting back with his wife. As this destructive thought entered his head, he knew it wasn't true. The years of neglect and grumpiness he'd inflicted on his wife were what prevented them getting back together. What a fool he'd been. Still, he'd turned a corner and he was going to enjoy today.

With plates piled high they made their way to a quiet corner of the garden. It was a lovely afternoon. The sun was warm, the food was excellent and he and his children were enjoying catching up. He looked away when he saw Jess kiss Gerald by the barbeque, but before he did, he noticed that they were the same build and similar height. No longer was she having to put up with a giant, slightly uncoordinated oaf. She would always be his wife, as far as he was concerned, but he knew he must be grateful that she was allowing him back into the family. Lots of their old friends came to say hello and even her mother spent half an hour with them.

Then his telephone rang. It was Sergeant Willis.

'You got a minute, Sir?'

'Not really, Sergeant.'

'This is important. A Gerald Hake was a former boyfriend of Anne Curry. They had a row in a restaurant in 2010 and the police were called. Isn't that your wife's new partner?'

'Thank you, Sergeant for letting me know. We'll have a chat about it on Monday.' He stuffed the phone back in his pocket.

'You okay.?' said Will. 'You've gone all white.'

'I'm fine son,' he said and put his arm round the boy's shoulder. 'It's so good to be here,' but his mind was in overdrive. Was Gerald dangerous? Would he harm his wife and children? What should he do? He couldn't warn them and he knew without doubt that someone was going to have to interview Gerald. The garden was emptying and Jess walked towards him.

'I'm glad Gerald treats you well,' he said to his children. If there was anything wrong surely they'd contradict him.

'Oh he's okay,' said Charlie.

'He's nice,' said Will, 'but we'd rather you still lived here.'

Nick struggled up from his seat to greet Jess.

'Looks like we'll be packing up soon,' she said.

'Oh yes, of course. I've had a lovely day and thank you both so much for inviting me.' He went to kiss her cheek, but saw her back away, so he awkwardly held out his hand.

'Thanks again.' He hugged the children and went to say good-bye to Gerald.

On Monday he had many things to sort out. After the briefing session in the incident room, he and Chris grabbed their notes and headed for the car.

'Right we're heading for Gerald Hake's office,' said Inspector Winsford.

'That's really not a good idea, Sir. I strongly advise you not to be the one doing that particular interview. If you discount him as a suspect, people will think it's because of your connection to him, and if you think he's in the frame, then people will think you're jealous. I know it's not my place to say but you should've informed the Chief of your connection.'

Inspector Winsford continued to walk in silence to the car.

Chris Willis tried again, 'I think we should visit 17 Park Road and speak to this Adrian Curry. Why didn't he report his mother missing? He might be able to answer the question of who the latest boyfriend was. There might be someone more likely as a suspect. I mean Gerald Hake's not got a record and the row in the restaurant was reported by the owner who was worried about losing customers. There's no evidence of any violence.'

Winsford held up his hand.

'Okay, Sergeant you win. Let's go and see Adrian Curry.'

Number seventeen was an end of terrace Victorian house with a small square of garden at the front. Although not well kept, it was reasonably tidy. There was a lack of both flowers and rubbish. As soon as they opened the gate a dog started barking. The door opened and Inspector Winsford introduced himself and Sergeant Willis as they held their cards out for inspection.

Adrian held Rusty's collar, while they made their way through to the kitchen at the back of the house. There were several candles stuck on saucers and in the corner was a single camping gas stove with small cylinder. It looked like the main utility services weren't being used.

Inspector Winsford looked at Sergeant Willis and could tell that he recognized that Adrian was the anonymous caller.

'Now son, sit down. I'm afraid I've some bad news for you.' he waited until Adrian had pulled up a stool to the kitchen table. 'A body was found in Viking Woods and has been identified as your mother, Anne Curry. I'm so sorry.'

Adrian's head drooped. 'I wondered where she'd got to.'

'You didn't think of reporting her missing?'

'I couldn't. Anyway she was always going off.'

'Why couldn't you report her missing Adrian?' asked Sergeant Willis.

The boy looked up at him, 'I was fifteen when she scarpered. They'd 'ave taken me into care. I'm eighteen now so no-one can touch me.'

'That's right. No-one can put you in care now son, but we would like some help in catching her killer.'

'I don't know nothing. She went out to see 'er bloke and she never came home.'

'I don't suppose you know the date she left. It's a lot to ask you Adrian after all this time,' said Sergeant Willis.

'Yeah I do know. It was 14 February 2012. I think she was going out for a romantic dinner with that guy from the garage down the road, Mick something. He 'asn't seen her though, 'cos he asked me where she'd got to.'

'That's really helpful. Did he ask on 14 February or was it later?' said Inspector Winsford.

'Later. I don't know when.'

'So, this Mick from the garage, was he the latest boyfriend, Adrian?' said Sergeant Willis.

'She had two blokes on the go. There may've been more. The other one was a poncy git, Gary or Gerald. Something like that. He had a nice car though.'

'Did this Gary or Gerald know about Mick do you think?'

'How the hell would I know!'

'Just one more question before we go, son. Did you get on well with your mum?'

Adrian looked at Inspector Winsford directly in the eyes.

'No, she was a shit mum. After Dad left there were all these blokes she brought home. The house only got cleaned when a new one came. There was never any food in the house and I couldn't bring friends home as she was always as high as a bloody kite on something or other. No Inspector, I didn't get on with her.'

'And have you lived here on your own since she left, with no help?'

'Yeah. No-one knew and no-one cared.'

'I care', said Inspector Winsford. 'Are you all right now? Have you got a job? Enough food?'

Adrian sneered at the two men. 'It's a bit late now, but since you ask, I'm fine. I work at the supermarket. I get cheap food and I manage. I guess this house'll be mine now.' He smiled.

'I'd like to send round a family liaison officer to keep you company. It might help as you've just lost your mother.'

'No way. I 'aven't just lost her. She's been gone three years. I cope by relying on me and I don't want some do-gooder sticking their nose in. Just leave me alone.'

'Okay Adrian, but you could go to citizen's advice about the house. They'll help you sort it out,' said Sergeant Willis.

'What about your dad? Does he visit?' asked Winsford.

'Oh yeah, he drops in every now and again, but he doesn't stop long. I ain't seen him for a while.'

They turned to leave when Inspector Winsford asked, 'Just to rule you out, where were you Friday morning? Walking the dog in Viking Woods perhaps?'

'No, I was on earlys at work.'

Once they were back at the car, Chris Willis said, 'Poor little sod. Fancy being on his own at fifteen. It's disgraceful that no-one noticed.'

'I agree with you, Sergeant. He's was only a couple of years older than my Charlie is now. Gives me the shivers,' Nick Winsford said. 'And while we're chatting, I didn't appreciate you telling me what to do this morning Sergeant, but I've thought it over and you were right, so thank you. We'll go back to the station and you can take someone with you to interview Gerald Hake. We want to know what the argument in the restaurant was about, whether he knew about Mick and whether they'd split up, etc. Be discreet where you question him but any form of non-cooperation, bring him in for questioning.'

'Yes, Sir and are you going to see if you can find Mick?'

'Hmm, yes,' Winsford said as he pulled out to join the traffic.

'Can we talk while I work?' said Mick Andrews when Winsford arrived at the garage. 'I've got a shed load of work on at the moment.'

'Sure,' said Winsford as he pulled up a stool and sat down close to where Mick was working. 'Can you tell me when was the last time you saw Anne Curry?'

'Not for ages. It must be years, 2012 or was it 2013? No 2012, I think. We were meant to meet up on Valentine's Day but she never showed.' He slid out from under the car. 'Why're you asking?'

'I'm sorry to tell you, Sir, but she's been found dead in Viking Woods.'

'Well that's a real shame. I thought she'd just gone off for a bit. She was always doing that. That poor kid used to be on his own a lot. I bought him pie and chips a couple of times.'

'Calling social services might have been more helpful.'

'I don't interfere. He was doing all right. I saw him go to school and get work. So what happened with her?'

'We're just trying to establish that. There'll be DNA at the crime scene. They can get trace DNA nowadays but it'll take a few days. We'll get the person who did this. Now were you her only boyfriend at the time of her disappearance?'

Mick pulled a face. 'We didn't have that sort of relationship. We were mates. We got together, if you know what I mean, when we'd nothing else on. I really never knew what she was up to. Didn't bother me.'

'Tell me about 14 February 2012. Take me through the day.'

'Normal as far as I can remember. We were going for a meal that evening, at the Italian on the High Street. She phoned me the day before said she'd come into some money and she'd treat me and she'd tell me her plans.'

'Where did the money come from and what sort of money?' said Inspector Winsford.

'No idea, but I reckon it was quite a few bucks. She was well pleased. Happy like I hadn't heard her before.'

'Did you ever meet a Gerald Hake?'

'Not so as I remember.'

Back at the station, Chris and Nick sat down with mugs of coffee and compared notes.

'So from the son, we found out that his mother didn't look after him after the dad left. Also that she had boyfriends in the plural. Mick Andrews confirmed those things and added the motive of money although we don't know where it came from,' said Nick.' We also learned there is a Mr. Curry, who's around now and again.'

'And from Gerald we've learned he was unaware of other men in Anne's life. They rowed over Anne's use of hash and only went out for a couple of months and then split up. He claims to know nothing about any money,' said Chris.

'We need to go back to Adrian and ask if he knew about the money and get onto her bank and see whether it's there.' At that moment Nick's phone rang. 'Excuse me,' he said as he walked into his office.

'Nick, how could you try and frame Gerald for murder of that girl? And after we've tried to be decent to you.'

Oh he didn't need this. 'Now Jess, you were married to me long enough to know that people known to the victim have to be interviewed and that I couldn't discuss it with you.'

'Rubbish, we were married for fifteen years. Of course you could tell me. We welcomed you into our home.'

Nick took a deep breath. It was his home. He'd paid the mortgage for all those years but he knew better than to say that.

'I know you're cross with me Jess for being a lousy husband, but when you've had time to think this through, I think you know I'm a good, honest, straight copper, for all my faults. I haven't fitted Gerald up and I never would. I need to get on. Give my love to the kids.'

It was at times like these he really felt the need for a drink, but he'd have to settle for a strong black coffee. Making his way back to the incident room he met up with Chris, who looked at him sympathetically. *Great,* he thought. *He must have heard me through those flimsy walls.* He needed to get back to work.

'We need to find out where Adrian's dad is living. He needs questioning. Come on. Let's go and visit Adrian to see if he knew about the money and bring that picture of the CCTV footage,' said Nick.

Chris nodded. 'Do you think Adrian killed her, Sir?'

'If he did, he's held it together extremely well since for someone so young, but maybe he knows more than he's told us.'

As they pulled up to the house they could see Rusty wandering around the front garden. He greeted them enthusiastically, as they made their way to the front door.

Inside the house seemed untidier than the previous time.

'She never had no money. I should know,' said Adrian, when they questioned him. 'There was never any food in the house.'

'On the day before she disappeared, she told Mick from the garage, that she'd come into some money,' said Inspector Winsford.

'Well she never told me. Where would she get money from?'

'Fair enough, but there's one more thing you can help us with Adrian,' said Sergeant Willis. 'On the morning your mother's body was found, you told us you were at work early.' He pulled out the picture of the caller from his pocket. 'So this image we have of you coming out of the phone box, where the anonymous caller informed us of a human bone being dug up, isn't of you.'

Adrian took the picture and stared at it. 'Look Rusty dug up the bone. I just didn't want the hassle of talking to the cops. No law against that is there?'

'Well son, it's a bit of a coincidence you being related to the body you found. I think we need to finish this interview down at the station,' said Inspector Winsford.

'Don't worry about Rusty, we'll make sure he's taken care of, Adrian,' said Sergeant Willis.

'Look I hated my mum. She was a right bitch, but I didn't kill her. You don't kill your own mother, whatever she's like.'

'Can you tell us your dad's whereabouts? We do need to talk to him.' said Inspector Winsford.

Adrian's eyes flickered towards the stairs. Nick nodded towards Chris but before he could move there was a thud, thud, thud sounded as someone started to come down the stairs.

'Who's in the house with you, Adrian?' said Sergeant Willis.

'I'm his dad,' said the stranger, who appeared in the doorway. He was tall and strong with a large belly and stank of stale beer and sweat. 'Jonathan Curry.'

'How long have you been here?' said Inspector Winsford.

'This time, two days, but I've been visiting on and off for the last three years. Yeah, since my wife died. He didn't know about the money and yes it was a coincidence he found her body. That's all it was.' He sat down on the grubby sofa. 'I left Anne when he was a little un. I was a useless dad, but I saved a bit, so he could go to college. I put it in her name 'cos I didn't want him wasting it.

'Your son is a major suspect in the murder of your wife. Is there anything you want to tell us Mr Curry?'

Jonathan Curry sighed. 'The day I brought the passbook round I went to the loo and I heard Anne on the phone to her bloke. She said she'd come into some money. I didn't save it for her. I just lost it.'

'Before you continue Mr Curry, I'd like to caution you,' said Sergeant Willis. When he'd been duly arrested and cautioned Inspector Winsford said, 'Please continue.'

'Sorry Adrian, I didn't mean to kill your mother. It was over in a minute. I took her up to the mound in the woods where we used to go before you were born. Thought she'd like it up there. The pass book's here,' he said taking it out of his back pocket and placing it on the stained coffee table. 'Adrian never knew anything. I just turned up again and told him I needed a bed but I didn't want the world to know I was back. I tried to be the parent I never was, but I never managed to stay long.'

'And how did you get her up to the mound?' said Inspector Winsford. 'There's no way a car can get up there.'

'Well I had to get her out of the house before Adrian came back from school, so I wheeled her up there in my mother's old wheelchair. I stuck a blanket round her and scarf and anyone looking would've thought I was taking a sleeping old lady for a walk. I waited up there until it was dark and then dug a hole to bury her in.'

'Time to go, Mr. Curry and we'll need a statement from you tomorrow, Adrian. Will you be all right?' asked Sergeant Willis.

'I did it for you,' said Mr. Curry, looking at his son.

'No, you did it because you can't control your bleeding temper. You're worse than her. At least she weren't violent.' Then he turned to Inspector Winsford. 'I'm going to be fine. Get that bastard out of here.'

Adrian picked up Rusty's lead. 'C'mon boy. Let's go for a walk'.

Inspector Winsford followed the lad and his dog out of the house.

'You know son, whatever type of mother she was, she didn't desert you. Perhaps that's something to hold on to.'

Adrian paused, leant down and patted Rusty, 'Yeah, maybe.' He almost smiled as he strode away towards Viking Woods.

If you've enjoyed this book you might enjoy other books by Penny Luker.

Missing – *Short stories for adults*
Pebble on the Beach - *Short stories for adults*
The Mermaid - *Short stories for adults*
The Child of Time – Ghost and paranormal stories

The Truth Finder - *Fantasy novels*
The Visualizer
The Healer

Nature's Gold - *Poetry*
Autumn Gold - *Poetry*
Shadows of Love - *Poetry*

Children's Books
The Green Book - a gentle, magical story
Chapter book

Tiny Tyrannosaurus - a gentle, magical story
Chapter book

Pablo the storytelling bear - a magical
Chapter book

Desdemona. The dragon without any friends.
Picture book

Read more of Penny Luker's writing at:

www.pennyluker.wordpress.com

Printed in Great Britain
by Amazon